THE **SYDING**

ADVENTURES

SUNSHINE

AND

SNOWSTORMS

WRITTEN BY **3** MARY WEEKS MILLARD

DayOne

© Day One Publications 2013

First printed 2013

ISBN 978-1-84625-366-9

All Scripture quotations are from the **New International Version** 1984
Copyright © 1973, 1978, 1984

Published by Day One Publications
Ryelands Road, Leominster, HR6 8NZ

TEL 01568 613 740 FAX 01568 611 473

email—sales@dayone.co.uk

UK web site—www.dayone.co.uk

USA web site—www.dayonebookstore.com

This book is entirely a work of fiction. Some actual place names have
been used, but the names of all people and the villages where they live
are entirely fictitious.

Printed by TJ International

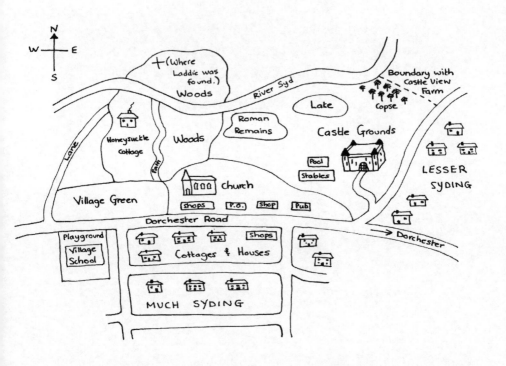

Map of Much Syding

Chapter One

Everyone at Lesser Syding Castle was excited. It was almost Christmas. The castle was home to four children and their mother, Sally. Penelope, the eldest daughter, was due home from boarding school that day. The thirteen-year-old twins, Sebastian and Felicity (Seb and Flick to all their friends) and eleven-year-old Theodore attended the High School in Dorchester, a nearby market town. They still had two more days of school before the holidays began.

Penny's train was on time and she greeted her mum with a huge hug. Within minutes the car was speeding along to the castle, Penny chattering all the way. She was glad to have her mother to herself before the others arrived home from school. They sat in the kitchen drinking tea and sharing news. Penny had won a scholarship to a specialist music school in Manchester and the family was very proud of her. A few weeks ago she had played a piano solo at a concert in London and her mother, brothers and sister had been able to attend and support her.

Suddenly, the kitchen door burst open and in ran Theo with his inseparable friend, Tyler. Theo hugged his big sister, almost squeezing the breath out of her.

"Hi sis! It's so good to see you again. This is going to be the best Christmas ever!" he said.

"It's wonderful to be home. Hi Tyler, good to see you again, too. How's your family?" Penny asked.

"We're all fine," he answered. "Dad will be round to collect me soon and he's bringing your Christmas tree. It's huge. You must come and see us. Sunshine is so excited even though she's too young to understand Christmas. She's walking everywhere now and we have a job to keep our eyes on her. She's talking, too. Mum never knows if it is English, Romany or just Sunshine language."

Everyone laughed. Tyler's little sister, Sunshine, was a favourite with them all.

"I'm dying to see the new river and the excavations and everything. Have you boys got time to show me?" she asked Theo and Tyler.

"Let's go now," suggested Theo. "It gets dark so quickly. We can take you on a proper tour as soon as we have broken up. We don't have any homework to do. Is that ok, Mum?"

Their mum nodded and Penny put her coat on. It was cold and had that wintery feel that made you think it could snow. The children ran through the fields to show Penny the new river. During the winter term the Ministry of the Environment had rerouted the river which ran through the castle estate, to lessen the danger of flooding to neighbouring farms and cottages.

In doing so, they had created a lake with an island. The family was now hoping to make a wildlife sanctuary and had planted a wild flower meadow. In the process of excavating the new river bed, Roman remains had been discovered. At the moment these were just fenced off, but work was due to start in the new year to excavate them.

Penny was pleased to see everything, but it was too cold to stay out for long. Theo looked after the hens and ducks which needed to be shut up safely for the night. As the three of them rounded them up, they heard the sound of Tyler's dad's Land Rover arriving. It seemed like the twins had hitched a lift up the drive with him. (They stayed on at school for various activities, so always were later home than the two 'T's', as Theo and Tyler were called).

"Hi there!" Bill, Tyler's dad, called. "Come and help me get the tree off the trailer and into the house."

All five children helped. It needed them all to manage the tree into the waiting bucket and then into the lounge. Theo looked at it in amazement. It must be the biggest tree they had ever had! They would need the ladder to decorate it. It had such a wonderful smell of pine needles, the sort of Christmas smell that you would always remember.

After much laughter they had the tree in place. The box of decorations looked a little inadequate for such a big tree so Penny promised that she would bake some cookie decorations the next day and possibly go to Dorchester to buy ribbons and make bows.

"First of all you need to put the lights on it!" she said to the boys. "As soon as you have had supper we'll start." They nodded in agreement and then remembered to thank Bill for bringing the tree to them before he and Tyler left for home.

Chapter Two

*M*ost of Syding Castle had been built in the eighteenth century, but there were a few parts which remained from a much older, Tudor manor house. The most spectacular of these was the great hall. The family now used it as the lounge. It had a large inglenook fireplace which was rarely used. This Christmas, however, Tyler's father, Bill, had brought a huge log, an old fashioned Yule log, for the family to burn. Bill worked for the Forestry Commission as caretaker of Syding woods. He knew so much about trees and wildlife in general, and from him Tyler had inherited a great interest in nature and the environment.

The children had great fun decorating the lounge. They had scoured the castle grounds and Syding woods for holly, ivy and mistletoe. Penny had been to Dorchester and bought meters of red ribbon to make bows. The Christmas tree stood in the bay window and was now decorated with red bows and the promised star shaped cookies made by Penny. Penny had also decided that her brothers and sister and their group of friends should carol sing around the village. It took her a while to persuade the boys, but eventually, they agreed and she made them practice some well-known carols. With her mum's help they dressed up like Victorian children and then, equipped with lanterns, they went around Lesser

Syding village singing at every house. The inhabitants were so delighted and they were given hot mince pies at almost every house! The news spread to Much Syding and the next evening they were asked to sing there. It was a much bigger village so they could only manage the houses in the High Street. They ended up by running along the path through the woods to Honeysuckle Cottage where Tyler lived for a wonderful supper cooked by Gran on an outside fire. Even though it was a chilly evening, it was such fun nobody minded being outside. To round off the whole evening they roasted chestnuts in the embers of the fire. Penny looked at her brother Theo and smiled. If Theo had not made friends with Tyler when they were at the village school, then none of them would be here. She looked round at the families. How different they all were, yet what good friends they had become. Tyler's family were Romany gypsies, the Jenkins' family with Paul, Tim and Tessa were farmers, and her own family who had lost so much when their father left them were now making a bed and breakfast business work.

As she thought about it, Penny realised that the reason they were such good friends was because most of them had become Christians and that created a strong bond. She herself was still undecided. Something within her was creating a longing to find God in a real way, but something else was making her afraid to say 'yes' to Him.

The next day was Christmas Eve. It seemed as if the whole village was bursting with excitement. Almost all the families went to the church for a special service in the afternoon when all the children would be given an orange each. The orange was decorated and used to explain to them how much Jesus loved the world. Sunshine was longing to get hers. Tyler took her to the front to receive it and carried it back so that she wouldn't burn herself on the candles, but as soon as she could she grabbed the sweets to eat!

In the evening, the villagers gathered again for the carol service. The church was lit by red candles and it looked so beautiful. Penny thought the music was wonderful and everyone sang so heartily. The castle family walked all the way home to Little Syding, singing as they went. Before they reached home there were flakes of snow beginning to fall. Perhaps it would be a white Christmas! It rarely snowed in Dorset. Snow at Christmas would make it absolutely perfect.

The village woke up on Christmas morning to find a blanket of deep snow. Theo looked out of the window in his turret room and everywhere for miles around was white. It looked so different. He found it difficult to make out Castle View Farm where the Jenkinses lived. He wondered if the sheep were alright on the hill. He knew Paul had said they might have some lambs at Christmas or New Year. Thinking about that made him think about his chickens. He had better go and check on them. Theo pulled on his jeans and a thick sweater and ran downstairs. His mum was already in the kitchen.

"Happy Christmas, darling," she called when she saw her son. He ran over and gave her a big hug.

"Happy Christmas, Mum! I am just going to check on the chickens and ducks as it's so snowy," he answered. "They will need fresh water and food anyway."

"Good boy. Clear a little path for the chickens. They will slip in the snow," Mum added.

It was gorgeous out in the snow. The chickens and ducks didn't seem to mind it at all, but Theo did as his mum suggested and made sure there was a little path from the coop that the hens could walk on. He got carried away for a while and began to build a snowman. Then he realised his mum was calling him in for breakfast.

After breakfast everyone gathered in the lounge where the fire was roaring in the grate. The Yule log was well and truly burning. Under the tree were presents and it was time to open them. The children didn't expect big presents. Since their father left home and started a new life in Australia, money had been very tight. For a time it looked as if they would have had to leave their castle home and find a much smaller house in which to live, but with them all working hard and helping their mum to make a go of the bed and breakfast business, life had become easier.

As they opened their parcels, they squealed with delight. Seb and Theo both received skate boards, Flick some rollerblades and Penny a long black velvet skirt to wear when she gave her performances. The children thanked their mum so much. They had clubbed together to get her some perfume. Penny remembered the kind she always wore when their dad was able to buy it. Sally, their mum, had tears in her eyes as she thanked them. They also had some parcels from their grandparents and aunts and uncles and close friends.

For some years none of them had heard from their father, but then he surprised them all by coming to the concert in London when Penny had been performing with her school as a soloist.

After the concert he had given each of his children an envelope which he told them to keep until Christmas. Their mother had put them away and now, they too, were under the Christmas tree. Each child had a card with a fifty pounds note inside. They were amazed! None of them had ever held a fifty pounds note in their hands before. However, what was far more important than the money was the card which said, "I love you and am sorry that I hurt you by leaving. Please forgive me. With much love, Dad."

Chapter Three

The snow was so thick that the village roads were impassable except by tractor. The children put on their boots and had great fun playing snowballs and completing the snowman Theo had started. Penny forgot she was supposed to be almost grown up and joined in, having as much fun as the others. It certainly gave them an appetite for Christmas dinner! Afterwards, they sat by the fire and played games and then watched television. It had been a wonderful day.

Penny didn't know when she had enjoyed Christmas so much. She thought back to the time when they had first moved to Syding Castle. The others had been quite small, but she was old enough to remember it clearly. Her father had spent thousands of pounds having the house renovated, and it was all finished in time for Christmas. He was a very successful business man and there was no shortage of money. Anything the children asked for they were usually given. She had asked for a baby grand piano!

Penny laughed as she remembered. What a thing to ask for! Then, on Christmas morning, in the lounge and covered with a red cloth was her present. A baby grand piano! How she loved that piano! As long as she could remember she had played the piano. Even as a tiny child she had climbed up on her grandmother's knee and played her piano. When she was only four she started lessons and loved them. Practicing was a joy, never a chore. Penny had no idea from where her gift of music came. She knew it was a gift—her brothers and sister had no interest in music; neither did her cousins. Something happened to her when she played. It was as if she was taken to another world. If she played a wrong note, she didn't have to be told, she knew at once.

Her gift of music had cut her off from some of her friends. They hadn't understood when she wanted to practice instead of going out with them. They had thought she wasn't much fun and had teased and then bullied her. She didn't even mind being called names, when she went to the piano she lost herself in the beautiful music.

Everything had changed when Dad left home. No longer was there money for the private school she'd attended or for music lessons. From having everything she asked for, Penny had to manage with almost no pocket money, getting up early and helping mum do breakfast for the guests and then going along to the local school where she had no friends and had much less time to play the piano. At first, it had been hard and she had been very resentful. Gradually, life had improved when her piano teacher insisted she still have lessons even if there was no money to pay for them. She had worked hard and was so delighted when she'd sat for a scholarship at the music academy and had passed with flying colours!

The first term at the academy had been so good. She had to do ordinary lessons of course and was working for her GCSE exams, but there was lots of music. She had private piano lessons but also played the flute in the school orchestra and sang in the choir. All the pupils were there because they loved music and some had become her good friends. However, there was one problem in her dormitory. The girls had begun to play a game called 'Ouija' and wanted her to join in.

Although Penny wasn't a Christian, she knew that this game was scary and evil. She didn't want to join in but hated being called a 'scaredy cat' and made fun of by her dorm mates.

They kept telling her that she could find out her future or even talk to her granddad who had died two years ago. Didn't she want to know if she was going to be a famous concert pianist? Didn't she want to know if she would marry a handsome boy and have lots of children?

Penny didn't know if she did or didn't want to know these things. So far, she had got out of playing the 'game' by telling the girls she was friends with a gypsy and could have her fortune told at any time. She told herself she was telling a white lie. Although Penny had called it a white lie, she knew that there isn't such a thing. All lies are wrong, whether deemed small or large. Tyler's mum, Betty, had given up fortune telling after she became a Christian.

Penny gave a huge yawn. Her thoughts had been wandering around. It was time for bed. It had been a wonderful Christmas and she was happy. Maybe she should just say thank you to God and go to bed.

Chapter Four

*M*r Jenkins had cleared some of the roads through the village, spreading sand and salt from his tractor. It meant that people could walk to the shops or get the bus to Dorchester. However, there was still plenty of snow to play with, and the village children took advantage of that. The fields around the Jenkins' farm had some good slopes and Paul, Tim and Tessa had a sledge. They phoned Tyler and the castle family to come and join them. After much hunting in the outhouses at the castle, Sally found a wooden sledge which she had used as a child. She had been brought up in the borders of Scotland where most winters had been snowy. She also found a couple of trays which could be used as well. Penny had decided that she needed to practice the piano so she didn't go up to the farm with the others.

It was a fantastic place to sledge. The slope was just steep enough but not too steep to climb up afterwards. They had such fun. Even when they fell off the sledge into the soft snow it was fun. The Jenkins' dog usually came bounding over to them trying to lick their faces as if to comfort them.

When they were tired of sledging they decided to have a snowball fight. It had to be teams of three against four. Theo wished Penny had come to make the sides even. Everyone played for the sheer fun of it and they only stopped when they became too hot. To cool off the children then made a huge snowman, almost as big as the one at the castle. Then they decided to pelt it with snowballs.

Mrs Jenkins was well known in the village for her baking ability. She had made lunch for all the children, so around the large farmhouse kitchen table they tucked into hot sausage rolls and jacket potatoes with all sorts of fillings. Big mugs of hot chocolate with marshmallows on the top made a perfect ending to the meal and gave them renewed energy to go back on the hill and sledge some more.

After about three quarters of an hour, Flick had just climbed up the hill again towing her mum's old sledge when she thought she heard a funny sort of moan. It seemed to be coming from the direction of the hedge in the far corner of the field.

Flick thought she ought to investigate, so she wandered off to see what was making the noise. As she got nearer the hedge, she could hear the noise more clearly and it definitely was an animal in pain. She climbed the stile into the next field and found a ewe under the hedge. It seemed to be bleeding as the snow was red.

As she looked more closely, she realised that the ewe was trying to give birth to a lamb. All Flick could see was a hoof coming out, but looking at the ewe and hearing her moan, she thought something must be wrong. For a moment Flick paused and rubbed the ewe's head, not knowing what to do. Then she had an idea.

"Paul!" she yelled in the loudest voice she could make. "Paul, help! Bring my sledge over here!"

The other children were laughing and screaming so much that Flick wondered if they could hear her. Maybe she should leave the ewe and run down to get them to help? However, the Jenkins' dog had heard. He came bounding up, barking, and she sent him back to Paul.

"Get Paul! Get your master!" she commanded. The dog bounded away as if he understood, and she bent down to comfort the ewe who seemed very distressed. The lamb still had not been born. Flick stood up again and yelled once more and was relieved to see Paul running up the hill with the others just behind him.

"Paul, get my sledge!" she shouted and this time he heard her and went charging back down the hill to find it. When the others arrived they thought it was Flick who had been hurt and needed help but soon saw it was a ewe.

Paul took over. He had seen his father help the sheep and could see this lamb was coming out the wrong way and was stuck in its mother's womb.

"I thought we could put her on my sledge and take her down to the farm," said Flick.

"That's a good idea," said Paul. "Your mum's sledge is ideal for that. If four of us help, we should be able to lift her without causing too much stress and we'll pull her gently down the hill. We need to go to the gate at the other end of the field and down the long way. It will be easier for her. If she gets too distressed the lamb will die. It may be dead already, but we may save the ewe."

Paul turned to his friends. "Have any of you got your mobile with you?" he asked. "Mine is at home."

"I have," said Seb.

"Good," answered Paul. "Can I phone Dad and get him to meet us?"

They were able to get hold of Mr Jenkins, who was doing the milking. Then, the four boys gently lifted the ewe onto the sledge. Flick took off her anorak and covered the animal because she knew that is what should be done for a human casualty. The children gently pulled the sheep through the fields and were almost at the farm when Mr Jenkins arrived.

He was most concerned and laid the ewe down on the grass, put on a long glove and examined her. He turned the lamb around in its mother's womb and pulled it out the right way. It looked dead, but he kept rubbing it and rubbing it. Eventually, it began to breathe. Amazingly, it struggled to its feet and went to its mother to suckle.

"Well done! And thank you," said Mr. Jenkins. "You have saved both the lamb and the ewe! They are very valuable animals."

"It was Flick who heard her moaning in the top field, Dad, and she who saved her!" said Paul.

"Well done, Flick. I am so grateful," Mr Jenkins turned and smiled at her. "We had better call the lamb after you! I think Felicity is rather long, so we will call her by another name which means the same. We will call her Joy! Now, my dear, I think you had better put your anorak on again, or you will be the next casualty. Maybe we should all go to the kitchen and have some hot chocolate or something!"

The children didn't need any second bidding. They ran into the farm and were soon telling Mrs Jenkins about the ewe and the new lamb called Joy.

Chapter Five

*A*fter the others had left to go sledging at Castle View Farm, Penny settled down to do some serious practice. She quickly became absorbed in the music she was playing and hardly heard her mother call her for lunch. After she had eaten she decided to go out, as the sun was shining and the snow looked lovely.

Her mother suggested that Sparks the pony could do with some exercise. Sparks belonged to Tyler's gran. He used to pull her 'vardo' as a Romany caravan is called, but now he lived in one of the empty stables at the castle.

In the days when Penny's family had been well off, all four of the children had had their own ponies, so she knew how to ride well.

Penny changed into her riding gear. It barely fitted her now as she had grown so much, but the most important thing was that her hat still fitted. She saddled up Sparks, who was very lively and pleased to be going out. She patted him gently and talked to him before she mounted because he was not as used to her as he was to Flick, who usually took care of him.

They trotted down the drive and through the great arch which once held a gate into the castle. She then decided to ride into Much Syding as Mr Jenkins had pretty well cleared the road. Sparks didn't seem to mind the snow or the cold and both of them were enjoying the exercise. When they got as far as the village school Penny decided she would visit Tyler's gran. She knew she was always delighted to see her pony, and she also wanted to ask some questions about the Ouija board game that some girls were playing at school. The way through the woods was a short cut to Honeysuckle Cottage, and Penny thought she would risk riding that way. It wasn't that easy because the snow was deep. At one point she almost fell off Sparks because he tripped on a tree root which was hidden by the snow. He was a good, calm pony and didn't bolt. Penny was thankful for that.

When they arrived at the cottage, even though it was so cold, Gran was sitting on the steps of her vardo watching Sunshine playing in the snow. She was well wrapped up with a shawl over her coat. Sunshine was also dressed warm and looked like an Arctic explorer. She was trying to make a snowman. She had made some snow castles with her beach bucket and spade but had got tired of that and wanted to make a 'no'man'.

Penny left Sparks tethered to the vardo steps so that Gran could talk to him, then chattered to Sunshine and helped her make a snowman. They had lots of fun and even played snowballs. Sunshine called her 'Pen-Pen'. She seemed to give all her special friends nicknames. Betty came out of the cottage to see what all the laughter was about.

"Pen-Pen make me no'man!" said Sunshine. "And we play no' balls."

"That's lovely, but it is time for your nap now," said her mum, picking up her small daughter even though she was protesting loudly. "I've put the kettle on. How about a hot drink?" she asked Penny and Gran.

"Yes, please," they both answered and followed Betty into the cottage kitchen.

Once Sunshine was put to bed and the women were sitting around the table, Penny felt she could ask her friends the questions which had been troubling her.

"I hope you don't mind me asking you," she began, "but there are some things I am worried about and I think you might be able to help."

"Of course we will help if we can," replied Betty. "Tell us what is on your mind."

"It's what's happening at school in the dorm. I love it at school and of course everyone understands about how much music means to me. I no longer get bullied about that, but now the girls have started to play a sort of game at night. They want me to join in but something inside me keeps telling me that it's evil and I shouldn't do it, then I think I'm just being silly. The others all think its huge fun and call me a 'scaredy cat' and other things.

"Sometimes I feel it wouldn't do any harm to play it and if I played it once then perhaps they would leave me alone. It's called Ouija. There is a board and it tells you things about the future. I told the girls that I knew someone who told fortunes so I didn't need to play the game. I know I shouldn't have said that, Betty, because you don't do it any more, but I thought I could ask you. Is it just a silly game? Would it be wrong to take part?"

Gran and Betty looked at each other, wondering who should answer. Then Betty began,

"You are right, Penny. I used to tell fortunes and make a lot of money that way. Almost all Romany women have the 'gift' which they call 'second sight' and from an early age are taught to tell fortunes in different ways. When I became a Christian, everything changed. I realised I was using powers that did not come from God but from evil sources. It was a huge battle for me to acknowledge that what I had done from childhood was wrong and I should apologize to God and turn right away from fortune telling. At that time I just knew it was wrong. Later on, I read in the Bible that it is strictly forbidden for God's people to take part in such practices. God holds the future in His hands and all He plans for us is good and we should trust Him.

"When I stopped doing these things it was as if a huge weight had been lifted off my shoulders, though up until that time I didn't realize the weight was there. I guess I had carried it unknowingly all my life. I felt like a little girl again, happy and free. It was hard because it meant I had now lost my job. Soon after that your mother and I became friends, and she asked me to help out with the bed and breakfast guests when she was busy. So God gave me a much better job and a very good friend.

"Penny, be strong. Don't get involved with the game, even if the girls tease or bully you! You may think that playing once wouldn't harm you, but it is evil and you cannot play with evil and not be harmed. It would be like trying to play with fire yet not get burnt! That, of course, is impossible. Ask God to help you resist the temptation to ever take part. It's not worth it. It really is wrong to get involved in fortune telling, tarot cards, Ouija boards and any such thing!"

Gran nodded in agreement. "When Betty stopped, I was angry. We all told fortunes—that's what Romany gypsies do! She was turning against her people. Then I saw the difference in her life. She was happy and had a freedom I had never known. No longer did she and Bill fight, get drunk or cheat and steal as so many of our people do. It was then that I asked God to forgive me too, and I became a Christian."

Penny sat quietly. Deep down she knew her friends were right. There was one problem, though. She couldn't really ask God to help her to be strong because she wasn't a Christian. Several times recently she had been challenged and she knew she would have to make a choice. Did she want to let Jesus become the 'boss' of her life? Was she

willing to give all her hopes and dreams to Him? What if
He didn't want her to be a concert pianist but told her to
be a missionary or whatever? She definitely wanted to be
in charge of making the choices as to her career and things
like that!

"Thank you so much for answering my questions," Penny
said to the two gypsy women. "You have really helped
me and I shall think about it in a different way. Now, I
had better ride home before it gets dark. I shall see you
tomorrow at the Wildlife Society's pantomime!"

Soon Penny was back on Sparks and they were trotting
back to the castle. It had been an interesting afternoon and
deep down, Penny knew that all Betty had said was true. She
decided she would not play the Ouija board however much
her dorm mates nagged her.

Chapter Six

The day after Boxing Day it was still cold and very frosty. No further snow had fallen. The sky was brilliant blue and the sun shone. The children were very pleased. They had planned a meeting of their Wildlife Club in the morning, and in the afternoon the castle family was hosting a party for their friends, the climax of which would be the pantomime which the Wildlife Club had been rehearsing for the past few weeks. It was to be 'Wind in The Willows' and had been written by Seb with a bit of help from the others.

The children had formed the Wildlife Club after the river course had been changed and they'd had the brilliant idea of making a wildlife sanctuary in the castle grounds. The grown-ups had all approved the idea and even expanded on it, hoping eventually to make it a commercial business.

The 'Man from the Ministry', as they had called the representative from the Ministry of the Environment, had suggested that the children all keep wildlife diaries. It would provide vital information about all the animals and plants that already lived in the area. The children had been very enthusiastic about this, but over the Christmas period there had been so much else to occupy their minds.

After breakfast, once they were free, the children phoned each other and arranged to meet at the castle. Theo's mum had promised to provide lunch for them all so that they could also have a dress rehearsal for the 'panto' before all the other guests arrived. Penny was not part of the club, since she was away at school, but she said she would help her mum with the food and also promised to be at the rehearsal and play musical interludes in the pantomime. She wasn't at all sure what she had let herself in for, but decided that playing nursery rhymes or carols would do.

Everyone arrived, after slipping and sliding most of the way on the icy paths. They didn't mind. It was such fun being in the snow. Once they had settled in the lounge with their notebooks, Seb, as the eldest (by half an hour), took control.

"Let's one by one read out the list of animals and plants or interesting things we have seen. Then, I think we should go out and inspect the lake. The wildflower meadow will be under snow, so we can forget that. Everyone in agreement?" he asked importantly.

They nodded and began to open their notebooks.

"Why don't you start?" Seb asked Tyler, who was sitting on his right. "Then we can go round the circle and I'll end."

"Ok," answered Tyler and began to read from his nature diary. "I've been watching the otters a lot. There seem to be two pairs and they are very active. They mostly go fishing, but I have seen them eat frogs and even crayfish. It's funny, I have noticed that if the ducks, moorhens or coots suddenly all start swimming rapidly in the same direction, it is a warning that there are otters about! I don't know why that should be, because they don't eat them.

"Besides the otters I have been looking for animal prints. In the woods there are squirrels, rabbits, foxes and deer. I think they are roe deer. I meant to ask my dad to be sure. Then, the most exciting animal was the weasel. At first I thought it was a stoat but it was smaller and like a thin brown sausage. It moved very quickly so I didn't get a good look at it, but I did see its tail and there was no black spot like a stoat has."

Everyone was very impressed by Tyler's report. The next to go was Theo.

"I've been bird watching as much as possible," he said. "We have had some winter visitors. I have seen redwings and fieldfares in the grounds here. Then there are robins, blackbirds, bluetits, long tailed tits, coal tits, sparrows, magpies, crows and sea gulls."

Tessa was sitting next to Theo. Her contribution was quite different.

"I wondered what happened to some of the insects in the winter and dad told me to hunt in the barns and sheds. I was so surprised because I thought butterflies died in the winter, but I found a comma and a tortoiseshell with their wings folded up in the corner of the shed. Dad says they hide away in warm and dry places until the spring weather comes. Then, I was in the barn and guess what I saw? I saw a whole lot of ladybirds all on top of each other. Dad told me they hibernate like that."

"Well done, Tess!" said Seb, and she blushed with the praise.

As they went around the group, everyone had seen interesting things. Flick had noticed the teasels which grew by the river bank were loved by the tiny goldfinches and also that the pied wagtails were often out by the water, while Paul had been very excited to see another winter visitor, the brambling, who comes from Scandinavia, feeding in the woods eating the beech nuts on the ground. Tim had found some grass snakes hibernating in the compost heap. At first he had been scared, thinking they were adders, then he realised what they were and quickly covered them up again.

Seb told them all how he had been learning to listen to bird calls and also he had noticed that when there was scurrying in the bushes, if he looked carefully he could see lots of birds. He had heard a swan making a huge noise and found it was a whooper swan because it had a black and yellow bill.

Everyone was really surprised at the variety of wildlife they had seen and also at how much fun it had been, keeping their nature diaries.

"I had no idea so many creatures lived around us, even in winter!" said Seb. "I have really learnt a lot. Now I think it is time to have a drink and snack, before we go up to the lake."

No one could resist throwing a few snowballs as they walked to the lake. The snow was still crisp and white and fun to walk through. The lake was iced over. They saw some mallard ducks trying to waddle over the ice, slithering this way and that, and the children just giggled at their antics. They hadn't really expected it to be like a skating rink but there had been several days of hard frost.

"I wonder if we could skate?" suggested Tim. "It would be huge fun!" The others looked at each other.

"Will the ice hold us?" questioned Flick.

Paul made a big snowball and threw it onto the ice. The ice seemed pretty thick.

"You're the smallest, Tess," Tim said to his sister, who was only nine and very small for her age. "Why don't you try first?"

Tess wasn't at all sure, but her big brothers often left her out of things because they said she was too young, so she wanted to show them she was brave enough to try. She gingerly took one step, then another on the ice. Of course, Wellington boots weren't like ice skates and she had a job to stay on her feet. The ice did seem pretty solid so Tim joined her. Paul felt responsible as their big brother and told them to come back. Tess did and as she reached the bank she heard a crack behind her.

"The ice is breaking! Tim, look out!" she called. A crack was opening up behind her. Tim looked around. Fortunately, he was still on solid ice, but he felt panicky.

"Try to walk carefully around the area cracking and as soon as you are near enough, jump to the bank," called Paul to his brother. The others all looked in horror, and Tim slithered on the ice. Much to everyone's relief he made it safely to a place from where he could jump to the bank. They all clapped when he was safe.

"Thank goodness! Don't ever do such a stupid thing again!" said Paul. "You hear stories of children getting killed when they fall through ice on ponds."

"Sorry," said Tim, who was really quite shaken. "I didn't think. It just seemed a fun thing to do."

"At least no harm's done. Let's forget it and have a race for home. That will warm us all up!" said Seb. They arrived back at the castle out of breath and laughing as one after another fell in the soft snow.

Chapter Seven

After lunch, the dining room in the castle had to be turned into a makeshift theatre ready for the pantomime. It was easy enough to clear a large space for a stage and arrange the chairs in rows, but very difficult to think how they could have some curtains. They needed somehow to make 'wings' where they could change costumes etc between scenes. In the end the children managed to tie ropes and hang blankets over them. It was better than nothing.

The costumes were pretty simple, sweaters and trousers in animal colours and masks made by the children. The script had been written mostly by Seb and Flick. They had both loved the story of *The Wind in the Willows* ever since they had been old enough to read it. Paul was very good at telling jokes, and he had made up some to make the story more of a pantomime. By the time he had finished, you could hardly recognize the original story, but no-one minded.

Once the theatre was ready, the dress rehearsal began. Penny, as she had promised, was helping with the music. She was using her flute because the piano was in the lounge and far too heavy to move.

The rehearsal was a disaster. Nobody remembered their lines and the jokes didn't sound funny at all.

The cast were looking pretty gloomy. The audience would soon arrive and what had once seemed a very good idea was now proving to be anything but good.

"One thing I have learnt since I have been at my new school," said Penny, trying to cheer them up, "is that the dress rehearsal is usually terrible, but the event is always much better. I am sure you will be fine. Let's add a few songs which the audience can join in and it will all go with a swing, I'm sure."

They decided to use a few songs from the musical *The Sound of Music* as most of the children had learnt them at the village school the previous year. Penny was really gifted in the way she managed to make the children sing like a choir. Soon the cast cheered up and were more like themselves.

Then guests began to arrive. Mr and Mrs Jenkins came from Castle View Farm. Next came Tyler's parents, Sunshine and Gran. Also, the elderly gentleman, Sid, from Little Syding who helped with the garden at the castle came with his wife, Edie. First, everyone sat down around the large kitchen table for a party tea.

What a tea it was! There were so many good things to eat! There was lots of fun and laughter. At the end, everyone pulled a cracker and by the time they were all wearing their silly hats and had told the silly jokes, even the cast of the pantomime had forgotten their nerves!

They all trooped into the dining room and behaved as if they were going to an expensive theatre in London. Seb announced to the audience:

"Are you sitting comfortably? Then I shall begin!"

He explained about the Syding Wildlife Society and how they had decided to perform a wildlife pantomime. He told the audience to sit back, relax and enjoy! Penny began playing some music and then got everybody singing a song that began, "Let's start at the very beginning, a very good place to start."

It was a hit! Tyler's mum and dad were very good singers and had often performed together, so they were able to give the singing a good lead. After that good start the pantomime began. Penny had been right—things were much better on the night. The cast remembered their lines and the audience shouted back in just the way they were supposed to—"Oh no, he isn't!" in all the right places. They also laughed at all the jokes as if they were the funniest they had ever heard.

In the interval Sally produced popcorn and ice creams. Not that any one was hungry, but they were irresistible. Penny played some music throughout this break, and when everyone had finished eating she began to play more songs, starting with 'My Favourite Things'. Her idea of audience participation in community singing was a hit.

The second half got underway and all went well until Tess got tangled up with the blanket curtain and pulled it down on top of herself and Flick who was waiting in the wings.

Everyone laughed and cheered and gave her a great clap. They thought it was all part of the act. Somehow the cast managed to keep going without too much giggling to the end, and when Seb finally announced, "So this is the end of our tale," wearing his badger mask and glasses which were too large and fell off his nose, everyone cheered and clapped as if it was the best pantomime ever produced.

They then ended by singing the song "So Long, Farewell" before taking their bows.

It had been such a lovely party and all the families enjoyed it. To think a year ago they hadn't even known each other! The old gardener Sid Frampton and his wife Edie said it had made their Christmas as they rarely had any visitors or went out. They loved seeing the children act. They loved joining in the singing too.

When Theo finally climbed his one hundred stairs to his bedroom, he was almost too tired to get ready for bed. What a day it had been! How well the Wildlife Society had done! Who would have thought there were so many species of birds and animals living around them? What would it be like when they finally had their own wildlife park up and running? Then he thought about the ice. It could have been a terrible accident. He quietly thanked God for keeping Tim and Tessa safe and prayed they would all be sensible. Then he said another thank you for the party and all the fun, especially that he had remembered all his lines and everyone had loved the pantomime. He yawned, snuggled under his duvet and fell fast asleep.

Chapter Eight

The Christmas holidays flew past and soon the children were thinking about getting ready to start the new term. The snow and ice continued, so every day when possible they met up to sledge or play snowballs. At New Year the castle reopened for guests. They were surprised to have six people booked in. Sally was glad that she had Penny at home to help her. Although it was hard work looking after guests, it was also exciting as the family were always meeting interesting people. Sometimes people liked to come again and again. These people became friends.

One such person was Mrs Samways. She arrived quite late on New Year's Eve along with her son Norman, whose nickname was Sam. Theo was delighted to see him again. It was the first time since the adventure when they had found him as a tramp along with his dog Laddie. They had so much to talk about. Sam had run away from home when he was just a boy, then lived with gypsies and become involved in an armed robbery. His mother had never stopped loving him or hoping he would someday return. Theo and Tyler had been instrumental in his being reunited with his mother.

As soon as Laddie saw Theo, he bounced over to him and licked him thoroughly, wagging his tail. He hadn't forgotten the boy who had rescued him. Normally, pets were not allowed to come with the visitors to the castle, but Sally had made an exception for Laddie so he was being housed in one of the old stables. Theo had made a warm bed for him from bales of straw and covered it with an old picnic blanket. He had put a bowl of water and a bowl ready for whatever food Sam had brought for him. Laddie seemed very happy in his temporary home when Theo and Sam shut him in for the night.

The other guests were a young couple who wanted to welcome the New Year in a quiet location because they were both very busy doctors who had worked all over the Christmas holiday in a big hospital in Southampton. The husband was a heart specialist and his wife was a surgeon who specialised in children's orthopaedics. The very cold weather, ice and snow had meant many casualties for both of them. Sally allocated them the best bedroom suite in the castle, well away from all the children's rooms. She hoped they would get the peace and quiet they needed.

The other two guests were a couple who loved astronomy. They hoped the weather would stay cold and dry so that they could star gaze. They lived in London and explained to the children that the orange street lights made it difficult to see the stars. It was called 'light pollution', a term that was new to them.

Because it was New Year's Eve, Sally had provided drinks and snacks for her incoming guests and told them they would be welcome to join the family at five to midnight in the lounge to welcome in the New Year. She knew that Mrs Samways and her son would like to join them and felt it only fair to ask the others.

It was the first year that Theo had been allowed to stay up to see the New Year in and he was very excited. He and Seb made up the fire. The huge log which had been placed on the fire earlier was still burning. Penny had gone to the piano and was ready to play 'Auld Lang Syne', the traditional song that everyone loved.

All the guests took up the invitation to join the family. Sally had bought some non-alcoholic elderflower champagne for the children, and they felt very grown up as they toasted the Queen, the country and each other's health.

They sang 'Auld Lang Syne' together, linking arms. When they had finished singing, Penny began to play it again.

"Let's sing the Lord's Prayer version that Cliff Richard sang at the millenium," she suggested. With her lovely soprano voice she led those who knew the words in the prayer. It seemed a very meaningful way to begin the New Year.

Just as Sally was sending her children up to bed, Sam thought he heard Laddie barking. He and Theo went to the kitchen door and sure enough, there was a commotion coming from the stable. They ran over and opened the door and the dog came rushing out and straight over the paddock to the hen house. Theo ran after him, his heart in his mouth.

What could have happened? He was sure he had shut the hens in. Sam followed as fast as he was able. A horrible sight greeted them! A fox had somehow got into the chicken coop and had killed them all. It was such a mess, feathers and chickens scattered around the coop and drops of blood in the snow. Theo couldn't help it; tears began to roll down his face. He had grown to love his hens and always looked after them so well. Sam put his arm around the lad.

"It's their nature, Theo. It's what foxes do. I expect it was a dog getting meat for his pregnant vixen. They get very hungry when there is ice and snow. I'm so sorry. Come on now, you are cold. Let's go to bed and I'll help you clean up in the morning," Sam said as he led Theo away from the scene of carnage. Laddie had gone off chasing the fox.

"Don't worry about Laddie," said Sam, "He'll find his way back to the stable without any trouble. He's used to living outside, remember?"

A very sad Theo returned with Sam to the castle. Everyone was still up and waiting to find out what the disturbance was all about and all were then very sorry to hear the news. Sally reinforced Sam's advice.

"Sam's right. You can do nothing now. We'll clean up in the morning. All these things are part of living in the country and sad though it is, we have to take it in our stride."

The hundred steps to the turret seemed like a thousand as Theo slowly climbed them. He got ready for bed and climbed in. He didn't feel at all like sleeping. All he could see were the feathers, chickens and drops of blood in the snow, which had looked so eerie by moonlight. He tossed and turned and finally got up and looked out of his window. The moon was such that he could see for miles. There were millions of stars twinkling in the heavens. One seemed very bright.

"Maybe it is a comet," he thought to himself. "I wonder what the star which the wise men followed looked like?"

As he stood gazing up at the stars and thinking of the wise men, it suddenly dawned on him that Jesus knew all about his chickens. He remembered hearing a verse from the Bible which said God knew if a sparrow fell to the ground, and so He would know all about the chickens. Then he remembered that the verse went on to say that we are not to be afraid as we are worth more than many sparrows. It comforted Theo and he felt aware that God did love him very much. Theo took one last look at the stars and crept back into his bed. He fell soundly asleep.

The next morning he woke up late. He was surprised to see the sun coming in through the window. Usually, it was still dark when he got up. He wouldn't have to go and collect the eggs this morning, he thought sadly. Then he remembered that it was the first day of a brand new year.

There was something wonderful about that. Yes, he was sad to lose his chickens, but many people had to face worse problems. He prayed and asked God to bless him and help him not just for the new day, but for the year.

When he got downstairs, Theo realised he was the last one up. Seb and Flick had helped serve and clear the breakfast for the guests and Penny had cooked for them. They all looked at him with sympathy and wanted to help him cope with his loss. Penny made him an omelette while his mum made tea and toast.

"We shall need to get some more hens and maybe a cockerel too," his mum commented. "I'll have a word with Mr Jenkins and ask him when he is next going to the market. When you have eaten perhaps you can let the ducks out. Sam, bless him, has already gone to clean out the coop. I'm not sure if he needs any help. Laddie made his way back to the stable without any problem. I guess he gave the fox the fright of his life, chasing him away like that."

After his breakfast Theo went to let out the ducks. He spent a while talking to them. They were always so funny and in spite of his sadness he couldn't help smiling. Then he made his way to the paddock. Sam was there, and had almost finished cleaning up all the evidence of the previous night's carnage. Theo tried to thank him, but Sam said it was nothing.

"Look how you helped me when Laddie was injured." He reminded Theo of the time when they had first met.

Theo knew that it would be hard for his mum to pay for more hens, but they did need them to provide eggs for their guests. He suddenly thought of the money his father had given him for Christmas. He could use it to buy hens. After all, the hens were more than mere animals to him, they were really his pets. He ran to tell his mum his good idea. She hummed and haa'd a bit, but finally agreed that it would be a good idea if that was really what he wanted to buy with his money. Theo nodded vigorously. He was quite, quite sure.

Chapter Nine

Tyler's father, Bill, had gone to see Mr Jenkins. He was increasingly worried that someone was poaching the pheasants that roamed the woods. Several times he thought he had heard gunshots and since the snow had come, he had seen footprints which he did not recognise and also strange car tracks in the lane near the woods. Of course, the woods were free for anyone to walk in and enjoy, but poaching the pheasants was not allowed and there were notices to say that too in several places. Mr Jenkins also had some game birds on his land, and Bill wanted to see if he suspected any poaching.

"I am sure something is going on. It may be just a gut feeling, but my years travelling with the gypsies have given me experience. It worries me, not just because of the birds, but also many people use the woods and there should not be someone out there shooting," Bill explained to the farmer. "I have no proof, but wondered if you had noticed anything suspicious."

"Well!" replied Mr Jenkins. "I have been so busy lambing, that I can't say I have. Mind, there have been a couple of instances when I wondered if a dog had worried the ewes, because there have been some lambs stillborn and for no apparent reason. The snow was so disturbed with the footprints of the ewes and lambs, I can't say I saw any paw prints. Maybe we should get the boys to go out and look for prints; they are very good at tracking and pretty good sleuths too!"

"I could mention it to Tyler," answered Bill, "but the two 'T's' have such a nose for trouble. I guess if they all go together and in daylight, they can't get into too much mischief."

"Thanks for letting me know your suspicions. I will certainly keep my eyes open. I don't want to lose my pheasants, but more than that, I don't want strangers disturbing the flock at this time. I'll have a word with Paul and Tim, too. I'm not sure about Tessa. Mind you, she won't want to be left out," answered Mr Jenkins.

The Wildlife Society was delighted when they were asked if they would look for clues in the woods and farm land. There were also pheasants in the castle grounds, so they decided to include those in their investigations. They still had a few days before they went back to school.

First, they held a meeting to make a plan of action. Flick and Tessa both wanted to be part of this, so they decided to have two teams. The two 'T's' and Tessa would search the woods, while Paul, Tim and the twins would search the farm land. Then, whoever finished first would begin to search the castle grounds and the others join them as soon as they could. They all had mobiles with them and promised to stay together.

There had been a fresh fall of snow overnight and that was a good thing, because any tracks they found would be new. There certainly did seem to be quite a lot of footprints and animal prints in the woods, but it was a place where many of the Much Syding people took their dogs for walks. However, there were fresh tyre marks in the lane, a very distinct pattern, and Tessa did her best to draw the marks. She was quite good at art and made a pretty good job of copying the tyre marks. The boys looked carefully for footprints near the car tracks and did find several which all had the same markings. Once again, Tessa set to work to copy them.

"We should have plaster of paris to make impressions of these," she said. "Isn't that what detectives do?"

"Yes," replied Theo, "but it's a bit difficult in snow and we have no idea if these are important. Anyway, you've done a great job, Tess. It's better than I could have done."

Tessa beamed at the praise. Her brothers rarely praised her but just teased their little sister.

Tyler pointed out prints of squirrels, pheasants, robins and blackbirds, even badgers. It was all very interesting, but inconclusive. When they had decided they had done all they could realistically do, they phoned the team at the farm to see how they were doing.

Paul and Co were very excited. They had found quite a lot of tracks in one of the upper fields. There were no sheep in that field, which made the tracks even more suspicious. There were footprints and dog paw tracks, as well as bird tracks. Even if a dog walker had been there, they would have been trespassers as there was no footpath through that field. The most exciting find however, had been a cartridge from a shotgun. This had been carefully picked up and put into a plastic bag, in the way the boys had seen it done in detective films on the television.

"Can you draw the imprint of the shoe?" asked Tyler. "Tess has drawn the ones here by the car tracks. It would be good to compare them."

"If someone has some paper and a pencil, we'll do that before we go to the castle," answered Paul.

"Good, we are on our way there now," replied Tyler. "Over and out," he added, just as detectives did in films.

It was a long walk from one village to the other, but it had been too icy to use their bikes, so the team from the woods set off at a brisk pace. They were walking along the road because the pavement was so slippery when a four by four vehicle whizzed passed them, splashing them all with slush. The children were not impressed. Most people driving through the village were careful. They stared after the vehicle, not recognising it as a local one. The number plate was covered in slush so they could not see it properly.

Back at the castle they had a hot drink of chocolate before they went out into the fields again. The pheasants hid in the hedges and bushes right on the far boundaries of the estate, so it meant quite a trek. On their way they saw the gardener, Sid Frampton, tidying up in the kitchen garden area.

"Good afternoon, Mr Frampton," Theo called out.

The old man straightened up and smiled.

"Hello, Theo, and let me see, it's Tyler and Tessa, isn't it?"

"Yes sir," they chorused.

"We had such a good time at your party. Edie and I keep talking about all the fun and the pantomime. You did such a good job. We hope the folks who moved into the empty cottage next to us recently will be as friendly as you all are. Maybe they will be good friends for you."

"Are there children, then?" asked Tess.

"Yes, we couldn't say exactly, but Edie reckons there are three boys and a girl. Maybe you'll know when you get back to school. Edie took in some tea and biscuits when they were moving. I think she said the family were called Banks."

The children were interested in this news. It wasn't often that new people moved into Little Syding. Four children! That could be fun, they decided. They only had one more day of holiday from school, so they would soon find out because Tess was still at the village primary school and almost all senior children went on the bus to the local high school in Dorchester.

50

The team from Castle View Farm arrived about the same time as Tyler and Co. Flick had her 'nature diary' with her and a pencil in case they saw any interesting wildlife. She had used this to try and draw the marks of the shoe imprint. The two teams compared their drawings and were very excited when they realised they were very similar.

"They must be the same!" said Tess. "I know I am not the best at drawing, but they are so alike!" Everyone agreed.

"I am so stupid!" said Paul. "Why on earth didn't I think about it and take a photo on my mobile! I had a new mobile that takes pictures as my Christmas present and I didn't even think about using it! I was so excited about us finding a cartridge and then you asked if we could draw it," he said to Tyler. "I'll go up first thing in the morning if there's time and take a photo."

"If it's still there!" said Tim. "It might have gone if it snows again or if it thaws."

"Never mind," said Theo. "We have some pretty good evidence. At least we have something to show for our day's work!"

They hunted around the hedges and fields together but found no more clues. There was just time for a game of snowballs before the light began to fade. Tyler and Paul had been chosen to take the report of their search to their dads, and the gang promised to be in touch in the morning.

Chapter Ten

Sunshine had been put down for her afternoon nap as usual. However, she felt she was a big girl now and didn't want to sleep. For Christmas her daddy had taken away her cot and given her a proper bed, which had a lovely pink cover with a picture of Sleeping Beauty in the middle.

She pushed the cover away and slid out onto the floor. She then toddled over to the bedroom door and tried to reach the handle. She tried and tried, but just couldn't undo it. Sunshine thought for a moment and then she pulled over her little chair and climbed up. Good! She could reach the handle now. She opened the door and made her way downstairs, going down on her bottom as she always did because she found it easiest.

When Sunshine went into the kitchen, no one was there. Perhaps mummy was having a nap too or was over in the vardo talking to Gran. She saw her Wellington boots by the kitchen door and pulled them on. She wanted to play in the snow. How she loved the snow. She loved the 'no'man' Pen-Pen had made for her. She loved Pen-Pen, too. She wished she was here to play with her now.

The kitchen door was open a fraction. Her mummy often left it like that so that Gran could come in. The vardo door was also open and Sunshine could hear Gran and mummy talking. She began to play, making her snow castles, but after a few minutes she thought once again that really, she wanted Penny to play with her, so she had a good idea. She would go and find Pen-Pen.

Sunshine was too small to understand that Syding Castle was a long way away. Every time she went there it was by car and so only took a few minutes. She toddled off into the woods quite happy because she had lived almost all her life in the cottage surrounded by people who loved her and took care of her. Tyler often took her out to see the squirrels or listen to the birds. Like most Romany children, she loved all living things.

She went quite a way into the woods, her boots scrunching in the snow as she walked. Then she saw the tree trunk where she often sat with Tyler. She swept the snow away and sat down. Perhaps she was more sleepy than she thought.

"Well, Ma," said Betty to Gran, "I'll just slip over and check on Sunshine. She doesn't nap for so long now. Soon our quiet afternoon chats will come to an end!"

Betty was surprised because the kitchen door was wide open. She had left it only slightly ajar. Maybe a gust of wind had blown it, she thought. She went upstairs and saw Sunshine's door open and was alarmed. Sunshine was nowhere to be seen, and when Betty saw the chair by the door, she realised what her daughter had done.

"Sunshine, Sunshine, where are you?" she called, rushing from room to room in case she was playing in one of them. In the kitchen she noticed that Sunshine's boots were gone, so she immediately concluded that she had gone outside to play.

"Ma, Ma!" called Betty, rushing into the vardo, "Sunshine's gone. She climbed on a chair and undid her door and her boots are gone. Oh, Ma!" and she began to cry.

Gran as always was calm, even in this crisis.

"Betty, love. Calm down. You all did it when you were small. It's the nature of Romany children to roam. She'll have toddled off into the woods to play. Now first, let's have a quick prayer and then you phone Bill before you go off looking. She won't be far away. I'll go and wait in the house."

Gran put her arm around her daughter. "Father God," she prayed, "You know where Sunshine is. Please direct Betty to her."

As Betty started down the vardo steps, she heard a noise which made her freeze. Her throat went dry and she could hardly talk. She had heard a gunshot.

"Go! Run!" commanded Gran. "I'll phone Bill and dial 999." Even as she said it, Betty began to run, not worrying that she hadn't got a coat or anything.

In the woods Sunshine had seen such a pretty bird. The colours were bright and it had a long tail. She toddled over to it, calling, "Pretty bird, come to Sunshine," and as she did

54

a terrible pain hit her head. It made her fall over into the snow, then a nice dog licked her face and she fell asleep.

As Betty came running into the woods, all the time following the tracks of her daughter's boots, she was vaguely aware of a dog barking and then a vehicle taking off at speed. She came to the clearing and saw a heap on the ground. It was as if her heart stopped still and for a moment she didn't know what to do.

"Lord help me!" she cried silently, as she bent down beside the tiny body. Blood was streaming from Sunshine's head, spreading out on the white snow. To her great relief, Sunshine was breathing. Betty took off her jumper and wrapped it around her little girl, who also had no coat on. Betty felt in her jeans' pocket and pulled out a small packet of tissues. She took out a whole wad and pressed them against the wound to try and stem the flow of blood.

Tears streaming down her face, Betty knelt by her baby, afraid to move her in case she caused more damage, and prayed. As she prayed, Betty suddenly felt as if arms were around her, and the warmth of God's love filled her. She didn't even feel cold, although she was only in her underwear, and her terror lifted.

It seemed as if she had been there for hours, but in fact it was only about twenty minutes before she heard the siren of an ambulance or police car. Suddenly, the wood seemed full of people. First there was Bill, gently helping her off the ground, while paramedics and police took over. They wrapped Sunshine in a sort of silver paper blanket to keep her warm. Bill helped his wife back into her sweater and the medics put a blanket around her. They placed Sunshine on a stretcher. She looked so tiny as they carried her to the ambulance which was waiting by the cottage.

"Be brave, madam," said the paramedic. "You have done a good job stemming the flow of blood and keeping her warm. She's in the best hands now. The hospital is waiting for her. You can ride in the ambulance and your husband will follow us."

He turned to Bill, "Your wife will need warm clothes and an overnight bag and things like that so she can stay at the hospital. Follow us to Dorchester."

Within minutes they were on their way with the sirens blaring. The paramedic had put a drip into Sunshine's arm and told her worried mum that her pulse was improving.

Chapter Eleven

*W*hen the children arrived back at the castle excited with the results of their day's work of sleuthing, they were shocked to hear the terrible news that Sunshine had been shot. Gran had phoned Theo's mum as soon as the ambulance had gone to the hospital and told her all about it. She asked if Tyler could have his meal at the castle and Sally had suggested that he stayed overnight, or for as long as was needed.

She talked to Tyler and tried to calm him down. He adored his little sister and wanted to go to the hospital to be with her. Sally told him that just wasn't possible until the doctors had seen her and decided what to do. She told him she would make up another bed in Theo's room and he could stay at the castle as long as he wanted.

"No thank you, Auntie Sally (as he called Theo's mum). I can't leave my gran on her own. She isn't very well herself and she will need me. I will sleep in the vardo with her. Anyway, we have to go back to school tomorrow and I shall need my things. Can you take me home after we have eaten?"

"Of course. Whatever you think is best. We are here whenever you need us and the same for your gran. I asked her if she would like to stay here for the time being, but she felt she should stay by the cottage in case anything is needed. I do understand and I am sure she will be glad of your company. By the way," she added, looking at all the children, "don't go back to the woods. They are now cordoned off by the police and the only way to Tyler's house is by the lane.

"The police may be very interested in your finds, though, so when I take Tyler back I shall tell them that you have found a cartridge and prints. You may have vital clues. Now we are all going to eat together before your dad picks you up," Sally said, looking at Paul, Tim and Tess. "Go and wash and before we eat we will pray together for Sunshine. She is in the very best hands of all, the hands of our loving Father God."

The children were very quiet and tearful as they came to eat. No one really felt like food, but as Sally said, they needed to keep up their strength, carry on as normally as they could and also help each other, especially Tyler and his family, through the crisis.

After the meal, Mr Jenkins arrived to take his children home. They all had to get ready for school the next day. Then Sally took Tyler home. The area was full of police cars and she had to explain who she was and why she was going to Honeysuckle Cottage. The local policeman was there too and she was relieved when she saw him. She told him about the children's search that day for clues as to who might be poaching pheasants. He thanked her very much and promised to pass the information on to the Detective Inspector who was in charge of the investigation.

When Tyler saw his gran, he immediately burst into tears and she hugged and hugged him. Sally just waited quietly, knowing that a good cry would help both of them. She waited until Gran could tell her the latest news, before she left for home.

"Sunshine was taken straight to the operating theatre and Bill promised to ring when she came out. They warned him that it will take a few hours because the bullet is lodged in a difficult place. She has lost a lot of blood, but is having a transfusion and her condition is stable," Gran told her. "We must keep on praying for her."

"We will and for all of you." Sally gave Tyler a hug, then Gran and then drove home.

Back at the Syding Castle, Penny had retreated to the lounge to play the piano. It was where she went whenever she needed to hide from the pain she felt in her heart. She loved little Sunshine so much, as much as if she was her own sister. She had spent hours and hours playing sad music when her dad had left home. Penny knew it was a sort of escape from the pain, when she didn't know what else to do. It helped ease all the questions in her mind. How could God have let this happen to such a sweet child as Sunshine? It just didn't seem fair. Why did bad things happen to good people?

Half of her wanted to believe in God, but the other half was so angry with the way He seemed to run the world.

As she played, tears streamed down her face. She hardly knew what she was playing, but found herself playing 'Brother James' Air', a haunting tune to which they sang the twenty-third psalm at school. The words came into her mind and she sang, "The Lord's my Shepherd, I'll not want," and as she sang, Penny remembered how they had talked about Jesus being the Good Shepherd at the church youth group just before she had gone to boarding school. She tried to think where they had read about it in the Bible and remembered it was in the Gospel of John. She must read it again, she thought to herself. She remembered that it talked about the 'Good' Shepherd, and the leader had explained it was a name for Jesus, who gave his life and died to save the sheep. That must mean that Jesus had been willing to die for her. Did He really love her that much?

Once again she played and sang the psalm. Then, feeling comforted for the first time, she really talked to God from the depth of her heart.

"O God, I don't understand how this terrible thing could happen, but I know you are the Good Shepherd and little Sunshine is your lamb. I think you said you would carry your lambs. Please hold and heal her now. And me too. I feel so messed up inside, so unsure and sometimes so angry. Please forgive me because I haven't bothered about you and only really loved my music and my family. Also, please can you help me to be strong in the dorm and not play the Ouija board?"

Penny felt at last she had made her decision. She had handed over her life to God, even though she had many questions and worries. Deep down inside, she knew God had heard and Jesus was her Shepherd. She knew it would not be easy at school, but she had asked the Lord to help her. The next day she had to pack and she made a mental note to include a Bible. She must find that passage about the Shepherd too!

With these thoughts, Penny closed the piano and decided to go to bed. She still felt sad, but the pain inside was different. Somehow, she felt at peace too. She knew she had made the right choice, even though it had been a struggle to do so.

Chapter Twelve

Theo and the twins all felt miserable as they walked down the drive to wait for the school bus the next morning. Theo wondered whether Tyler would be on it or if he would take the day off to look after his gran.

To their surprise there were two other boys waiting at the gateway to the castle. They were quite big boys and scowled at the three children who had smiled and said hello to them. When the bus arrived they almost pushed Flick into the ditch as they made sure they were first onto the bus. Then, they were rude to the driver when he asked to see their pass, and the largest boy knocked one of the girls on the head with his bag as he passed up the aisle. He didn't even say sorry! Seb and Theo looked at each other. These boys looked as if they would be trouble with a big T.

"I wonder if they are the family who have moved next door to Sid and Edie?" Flick whispered to her brothers as they went to get their seats.

"I guess they probably are," replied Seb. "If they are always so rude, it will be horrible for them."

Theo was glad to see Tyler in his usual seat, waiting for him.

"Who are those boys?" Tyler asked Theo.

"We're not sure. We think they may be Sid and Edie's new neighbours. I hope not—they are very rude!" answered

Theo. "I wasn't sure if you would come to school today or stay and be with your gran," he added. "And is there any more news of Sunshine?"

"I wanted to stay at home, but you know my gran. She said the best place for me was back at my desk and to carry on as normal. As if anything could be 'normal' after what's happened." Tyler stopped a second to compose himself. He was clearly very upset. "Anyway, she said Dad would be back this morning and Mum would stay at the hospital, then he would go after work and Mum could come home for a rest. It seems Sunshine may have to be there for some time, so they will be with her on a rota basis.

"The good news is, that although it was a long and difficult operation, they removed the bullet. It had lodged in her brain. We will have to wait and see if it has caused long term brain damage, but Sunshine has woken up and talked to them both. She seems to be able to move her arms and legs and the nurses say that is a very good sign. I can go to see her after school and then come home with Mum."

"At break, let's go to the prayer space and put her name down so people will pray for her," said Theo. "God has done miracles for us before, so we can ask Him to do another one."

"Yes, I was going to do that. I am so tired; I hope I can concentrate today. You can pray for me, too."

It was good to see everyone in the year group again and hear all about their holidays, but both boys had almost forgotten all the fun they'd had, it seemed so long ago. The day dragged by and eventually Theo got on the bus to go home. He was glad to see Seb and Flick had decided not to go to homework club but come home with him. He didn't fancy getting off the bus alone with the two new boys who seemed very aggressive. Walking up the drive, he heard them call after the three of them.

"Fancy rich kids, we'll knock off their toffee noses!"

His stomach turned into a knot, remembering what it was like to be bullied when he was at primary school. Then they started pelting them with snowballs. It was no longer the soft snow but was icy and had grit in it.

"Take no notice," whispered Seb to his brother and sister. "The younger boy is in our class and he is called Cane. If he had gone to school a generation ago he would have got the cane too—he was even cheeky to Mr Woods in maths! He speaks with a Cockney accent. Maybe the move has upset them. Little Syding is a bit different from London."

As well as the news which Tyler had given Theo about Sunshine, their mum had heard from Betty and Bill that the surgeon was very pleased with the progress she had made but warned them it was still very early days.

"I have some news for you all too," Mum announced. "The Jenkins children are coming here and the detective inspector wants to talk to you about your sleuthing yesterday and the things you saw and found. He will come at five o'clock, so you have time to have a snack and get yourselves sorted out. Tyler is at the hospital of course, so he won't be here."

"We'll have an extraordinary meeting of the Wildlife Society with the inspector!" said Seb, who liked to do everything properly. "I will take notes and record it for our records. After all, we may help to catch a criminal!"

Penny had spent most of the day doing her packing, as her train left early the next morning. She had asked her mum for a Bible, and her mother had given her a lovely blue one with a zip around it.

"I bought it for you for Christmas but wasn't quite sure if you wanted one yet, so I just kept it in my room. I have been praying that you would want to find out more about God. Knowing Jesus as my Saviour and friend has made so much difference to my life. I have been praying that all my family would come to love Him too."

"Mum, I don't quite know how to say this, but last night with all that happened, I sort of asked Jesus to help me, and I know that although I am still upset and sad, I do feel different." Penny looked at her mum and could see she understood. "Thank you for this. I want to read about the Good Shepherd. I think it is in the book of John?" she asked her mum.

"Yes. I can tell you that. I am just a beginner, but I know that passage is in John, chapter ten," Sally replied, smiling at her eldest daughter.

"Oh, thanks a million!" Penny said and went to her room to read the chapter before she packed the Bible in her case. Then she went to the lounge and began to play 'Brother James' Air' again and sing the psalm to herself. In the kitchen her mother heard her and hummed along, happy that some good had come out of the terrible accident.

The detective inspector arrived at five o'clock precisely. All the children were waiting for him in the lounge. They were a little shy at meeting such an important person, and Theo was worried that he might think them silly, hunting for clues. However, along with the inspector was the local policeman, who knew Theo and Tyler quite well, having helped them with previous adventures. He smiled at Theo and said to the inspector, "I think we have a trainee police officer in this young man. He and his friend, Tyler, who is the brother of little Sunshine, have been a great help to me."

The inspector asked the children about the day they spent hunting for clues. He asked why they had gone out in the first place and Paul explained how his father, who was the farmer at Castle View Farm and also Tyler's father, had a suspicion that someone was poaching the pheasants on the farm land and in the woods. They suggested that the children go and look for clues. Seb explained how they were members of the Syding Wildlife Society and tried to monitor the animals, insects, etc. in the area.

He told the detective inspector how they had divided themselves into two groups and the girls produced the drawings they had made of the footprints, paw prints and tyre prints.

"Afterwards I realised we should have photographed them on my mobile, but I didn't think of it. I meant to go back before school this morning and take a photo, but all the worry about Sunshine drove it out of my mind. I'm sorry about that," said Paul.

The inspector took the papers with the drawings, studying them carefully.

"These are very interesting and you have done very well," he said. Flick and Tess blushed with the praise. "I am sure my officers will find them very helpful."

Then Seb produced the cartridge, still in the polythene bag. "We tried not to touch it with our fingers," he explained. "We had no idea, of course, that it might be needed for a police investigation."

"Well done!" praised the inspector. "I will have this forensically examined. We must catch the person who shot Sunshine. To shoot and poach pheasants is a serious crime, but even to accidently shoot a child and then leave and run away from the scene of the crime is a very terrible thing to do. Your help will be invaluable."

"Now, there is one more thing. I know it is dark now, but could one of you come with me to show me exactly where you found the footprints, the cartridge and the tyre marks? It means I can get my officers out looking for them first thing in the morning. I know you would like to stay off school and show me them, but that can't be done." He grinned at the children.

"I'll show you the evidence we found on the farm, and if Tess and Tim can come with us, it will mean we are all home together for supper. I promised I'd text mum when we were coming home because she didn't want us to walk back in the dark," suggested Paul.

"I'll show you the place in the lane where our prints came from," volunteered Theo. "But they may be gone now with all the activity around Honeysuckle Cottage."

"Never mind, Theo," replied the inspector. "At least we will know where they were, and it's amazing what forensics can do. If you go with your policeman and another of my officers, he can bring you back home afterwards."

The children got their coats and boots. It would have been really exciting if there wasn't the terrible worry about Sunshine. That hung over everyone like a terrible cloud. Sally found torches for Paul and Theo, and they all set off.

It was pretty hard for them to find the approximate locations, but they did their best. They would do anything to help catch the person who had wounded Sunshine.

Chapter Thirteen

Sunshine was very confused when she woke up in the hospital. All she could remember was the pretty bird. Where was the pretty bird? Why did her head hurt so much? Why was there a tube in her arm and lots of people wearing white coats? Everything and everyone seemed fuzzy. She couldn't see clearly at all.

Mummy was one side of her and Daddy the other, talking very quietly. It was a great effort, but Sunshine wanted to talk to them. Even the words came out in a funny way and didn't sound right, but mummy and daddy smiled at her and talked back. Their words seemed to be muddled up too. Perhaps if she closed her eyes and went to sleep, when she woke up again everything would be back to normal.

The doctors and the nurses were very attentive and kept reassuring her parents that Sunshine was doing well. Her condition was serious, but she was out of immediate danger. Bill and Betty quietly said thank you to God for that. They were aware that their friends were praying for their daughter, and that gave them peace and encouragement. The first night they were given lounge chairs so that they could both stay in the ward and maybe sleep a little. In the morning, once the surgeon had been to see Sunshine and told them he was pleased with her progress and she was stable, Bill left for work while Betty stayed.

When Sunshine opened her eyes that morning, things were much better. She could see and hear more clearly and her head managed to find words to talk to her mummy.

"Mummy, where has the pretty bird gone? Why am I in this strange place?" she asked.

"You went to see the pretty bird but had an accident, darling. Now you are in the hospital and will stay until you are all better," her mother answered.

"What is a 'osital?" asked Sunshine.

Her mum laughed. "A hospital is a place where you come when you need to get help to get better. The doctors and nurses take care of you."

Sunshine tried to think about that, but thinking made her head hurt. She shut her eyes again, that seemed to help make the pain go away.

After school Tyler went straight to the hospital. He was so scared to see his baby sister in a big bed with all sorts of tubes into her little body and monitors around her. She looked very small. He felt so angry inside that someone could hurt Sunshine and leave her for dead. If he ever met the person, they would be in for a shock. He felt as if he would tear them apart with his bare hands. He had forgotten what it was like to have all the fighting gypsy blood in him aroused. As a small boy, when the family were still living in

70

the Romany community he had started to learn to box from a very early age, as did most gypsy boys. Tyler looked at his mum sitting by the bed; she was so tired and pale. It wasn't fair. Why had God let this happen to his family?

When Sunshine saw Tyler, her face broke into a smile. "Ty, Ty, kiss Sunshine," she begged.

Trying not to touch any of the tubes or things, he bent over the bed and gave his little sister a kiss, then took her hand and stroked it gently. There had been times when he had thought his little sister a nuisance, but now he realised he loved her very much. All he wanted was for her to be better and back home. He would try always to make time to play with her. He thought about the rest of the gang and hoped that when they met the detective inspector, that their clues would be of use and help catch the person who had done this terrible thing.

After work, Bill arrived to stay through the night with Sunshine. He was delighted because he could see a great improvement in her condition. The surgeon came to see them before he went home and promised that if Sunshine was still doing well the next morning she could be moved into the main children's ward and have some of the tubes taken away. That made Betty and Tyler feel happier as they went home.

On the way home, Tyler complained to his mum that it just didn't seem fair that Sunshine had been shot. "Why does God allow bad things to happen to good people?" he asked.

"I really don't know the answer to that," replied his mum, "but bad things do happen equally to good and bad people. Being a Christian doesn't mean that life will all be plain sailing. I have learnt something myself through these past two days. When you are a Christian and something awful happens, you realise that Jesus is with you and helps you and so do the prayers of all your friends."

Gran was waiting for them and had cooked a lovely meal for them all. How fantastic his gran was. All day long she had been making cups of tea for policemen who were working at the scene of the crime and filling them up with her lovely biscuits, too. She told Tyler she was so pleased to have something to do rather than just sit in her vardo and worry.

Tyler phoned Theo to hear all about the meeting with the inspector and was pleased that the clues they had found were proving useful. He felt a lot better when he went to bed, but he did find it hard to pray because he had so much anger and hate towards the poacher bubbling up inside of him.

Chapter Fourteen

*P*enny went back to school and life began to take on a
more normal routine again. Tyler's gran was right—it
did help to do all the ordinary things every day. For Theo, he
was missing one of his 'ordinary things'. He had no chickens
to look after. The two ducks really didn't need much
attention. Theo had thoroughly cleaned out the hen house
ready to have some more chickens, but with all that had
happened in recent days, getting to market didn't seem that
important. He did miss his hens though and his mum missed
the eggs. Now they had to go the Jenkinses to buy eggs for
their guests' breakfasts. Maybe it was just as well that, after
the guests who came for New Year went home, they had very
few people staying.

At least the weather was warmer. The snow had gone and
although it had been such fun playing together, in the end
everyone had got tired of it. Now the Wildlife Society was
on the look out for signs of spring, even though it was just
January, because a few catkins had come out on the willow
trees by the river.

The best thing of all was that Sunshine was getting better.
Once she was on the mend, she amused the whole ward with
her chatter, still a mixture of English, Romany and her own
made up words. Sometimes she still had bad headaches but

was very brave and didn't complain much. Sometimes too she felt strange and then her body shook all over. The doctor explained to her parents that she was having epileptic fits. Until these were controlled by the right dose of medicine, she needed to stay in the hospital. The family were told that she might have these for the rest of her life, but once the medicine was working properly, they would be controlled and she would have a normal life. However, they were told, they may even disappear once the damage to the brain settled down. They learnt that if the bullet had gone any deeper into Sunshine's brain the outlook would have been very much worse. Everyone was so thankful for the way she was recovering.

A week or so after the accident, the police officer rang up to say that the detective inspector would like to come and see the children again. It was arranged that he would come on a Saturday morning and so another meeting of the Wildlife Society was arranged, once again at the castle.

He was smiling and greeted the children warmly.

"Hi, my young helpers!" he said. "I am pleased to see you again and say thank you for your very good observations. Your clues have been so useful to my team. With your help, we were able to find and match the footprints, and they are the same. The tyre prints also have been narrowed down to a certain type of four-by-four vehicle, one that isn't terribly common. That narrows down our investigation. I cannot tell you about all our finds, but I can tell you that the cartridge you found has matched the type of bullet that was lodged in Sunshine's head. That is very significant. We have our suspicions and our enquiries are still on going, but I am sure that because of your help we will catch the person responsible. Keep on the lookout for anything or anyone that is suspicious and let us know if you have any more finds. Mind, I guess the poacher is lying low for the time being. When he feels it is safe, he may start again."

"We certainly will keep our eyes open," Seb promised, and every one nodded. "We can watch our own properties. We are not going through the woods at the moment. It just doesn't feel safe."

"I have a wonderful lookout from my bedroom in the tower. If you like, I can show you," said Theo.

"That sounds interesting. Yes, why don't you show me?" the detective inspector replied. So Theo took him up the hundred stairs to his room. The inspector was quite puffed out by the time he reached the top.

"Wow! What a view!" he exclaimed when he looked out of the turret and could see for miles around.

"You have a fantastic view, and I see you have some binoculars, too! It will be very useful if you keep a good look out from up here!" he said to Theo. "And," he added, looking round the room, "well done. You keep it very tidy. My son could learn a lesson from you."

"I try to. Its part of the bargain I made with mum. I keep it tidy so she only has to come up and clean it every now and then. That way, I get to stay up here. If she wants me, she texts me, to save her legs," he added.

"Good idea! I don't think I'd want to keep running up and down all these stairs, although I might keep a bit fitter if I did," laughed the inspector.

Mum had made coffee for him and while he drank it the children talked about ways they could keep their eyes open and also about signs of spring. They all really liked keeping their nature diaries. Tessa struggled with things like spelling, but she made up for it by drawing pictures. Everyone admired her drawing of lambs' tail catkins, and nobody made fun of her spelling.

Before the Jenkins children went home, Paul had a phone call from his dad. It was actually for Theo.

"I don't know if you are free this afternoon, Theo," he said, "but I have seen an advert in the farming journal about rehoming battery hens. I thought I might go and take a look at them and wondered if you would like to come. If they are good stock, then you might get a lot more for your money."

"I've nothing special on," replied Theo. "Tyler is going to the hospital and we don't have any homework to do. Can I just go and ask Mum?"

Theo's mum was quite happy, so Mr Jenkins promised to pick him up as soon as the afternoon milking was finished.

Theo felt very grown up going to look at hens with the farmer. He asked his mum if he should take his £50 from his dad, but mum thought it best for them to see the birds, and if they were good, Mr Jenkins would pay for them and he could pay him back.

On the way Mr Jenkins explained to Theo about the rescue mission for hens. Hens reared in battery farms had no life at all. They were just like an egg-producing factory and were fed at one end, had no room to move and the eggs came out at the other end. Once they stopped producing well, they were discarded and now rescue centres had been formed so that the poor animals could go to good homes and be looked after. All of them were inspected by vets and treated if necessary. There was no charge for the hens, but a donation of £3 or £4 per hen helped the centres to keep running and pay the vets and food bills. As a minor, Theo wouldn't be allowed them in his own name but, sponsored by Mr Jenkins, he could have some. Mr Jenkins promised to keep an eye on the hens' welfare.

When Theo saw the chickens he was so excited. He really did love taking care of them and found they were really intelligent animals. He only had room in his coop for ten, but to think he had enough money for that many was fantastic. He could then buy some food with the remaining money to save his mum having to pay out.

He chose ten birds, and Mr Jenkins had twenty. It was good to think that thirty hens now had good homes and could run around scratching the earth and be free. The thought of them being egg factories had horrified Theo. The woman in the rescue centre was very helpful and said that, on average, they would lay about one hundred and twenty eggs a year. That seemed a lot to Theo. He would have a lot of egg hunting to do, he thought happily.

The hens were put into special cages that Mr Jenkins had brought with him so that they could travel safely in the back of his pickup truck. Before they were put into their coop, Mr Jenkins also looked at it very carefully to make sure it was now properly fox proof. When he was satisfied, the chickens were installed in their new home. Of course, when they were out roaming in the paddock, no one could be sure the fox would not get them, but mostly foxes do not hunt in the daytime.

"I think you may need a dog too," commented Mr Jenkins. "A gentle dog who will live happily with the hens and ducks but scare away the foxes. When the spring comes, I can lend you my cockerel and you can rear your own chicks. Then you can have chickens for food as well as for eggs. They are fun creatures, though they are not really pets but for food. Sometimes it is hard to remember that. Even I find it hard to send a lamb I have hand-reared to market!"

The thought of one day owning a dog was exciting. Theo loved dogs. Up until now his mum had said they could not afford to keep a dog. Food and vets bills were so expensive. He wondered if he could ask her again, now that more people were coming to stay at the castle. The prospect of rearing chicks was quite exciting too. He knew Mr Jenkins would advise him when the time came.

Seb and his mum came to admire the new hens and hear all about the rescue centre and proposals to rear chicks of their own. Theo even mentioned that Mr Jenkins had thought a dog would help guard the hens by day. Seb looked hopeful and his mum looked thoughtful at this suggestion.

"We'll have to think about that," Sally answered. "When the winter is over and we see how much money we have made, then it might just be possible. I know how much you would all love a dog, and it would be useful as a guard dog, too. We'll just have to wait and see."

Flick was out riding Sparks, so she didn't see the new arrivals. It was beginning to get dark and Sally looked anxiously at her watch.

"She should be home by now," she thought. After what had happened to Sunshine, she did not want her children out after dark.

Chapter Fifteen

After lunch on that Saturday, Flick decided to take Sparks for a long ride. He had been cooped up so much during the snow and ice and had not been ridden properly since Penny had gone over to visit Tyler's gran just after Christmas.

As Theo had gone to look at chickens and Seb and Paul had gone by bus to Dorchester to the skate park, it seemed a good idea to go for a ride rather than be at home with nothing much to do.

Sparks was excited to be going out, too. The stable might be warm and dry, but he was used to being out in all winds and weathers when he had pulled Gran along in her vardo. Flick had brought a carrot out for the pony, and he munched away on it happily as she put on the bridle and saddle. Soon the pair of them were cantering through the castle grounds thoroughly enjoying themselves. The day was cloudy, not too cold and dry, so it was ideal for a good canter. When they reached the new lake, they stopped and Flick looked to see if there were any new things she could put in her wildlife diary. Last time she had been at the lake was the day when Tess and Tim had almost fallen through the ice. She shuddered as she remembered. It could have been a very nasty accident. Now, of course, the ice was gone and there were mallard ducks, coots and moorhens swimming around. As she watched them, Flick could just see on the far side of the lake a grey heron. "I must remember to write that down," she thought. "I don't think we have seen a heron on the lake before, only on the river."

She decided to ride on to the very boundary of their land, where it joined the Castle View Farm fields. There was a small copse there and it was a good place to see birds and sometimes even deer.

She stopped by the copse and dismounted, leaving Sparks to forage for some grass while she walked through the copse. Suddenly, she was startled to see a couple of men. Then as she looked closer, Flick could see they were in fact boys. They were the two new boys who were so disruptive on the school bus and in class.

"Look who's here! If it ain't the toffee-nosed rich kid from the castle!" said the older boy, whom she now knew was called Jake Banks. The younger boy who was in her year group was Cane.

"Got some funny name, ain't she?" he asked his brother.

"Yeah, 'Flick'. What sort of a name is that?" Cane commented rudely.

"It's short for Felicity," Flick answered without thinking.

"Fel-i-ci-ty," mocked Jake, pronouncing every syllable in a mock posh voice. "That's a toffee-nosed name if ever there was one."

"What are you doing trespassing on our land?" Flick asked, quite angry now and a bit scared.

"Your land is it, then?" replied Jake. "So who do you think you are, Miss High and Mighty? I didn't see no notice about it being anyone's land. We come and go as we please, ain't that right, Cane?" he smirked at his brother.

"That's right, bro. There weren't any notice, as if we cared anyway. Well, there were that bit of wood we broke down, it said somethink like 'no tresspassers'. We're communists, ain't we, Jake, like our dad and Joe. They say the land belongs to us all, so we go where we like and take what we like!" Cane answered.

When they said they took what they liked, Flick suddenly noticed they had rifles. For a minute she went giddy.

Surely they weren't the ones, surely they wouldn't have shot Sunshine!

"You have no right here. I will report you to the police," Flick said boldly. Cane looked a bit afraid, but his brother began to bully Flick.

"Oh no, you won't. One word from you and your life will be hell from now on, in school and out. We know how to terrorise people, we have ways and means, ain't we, Cane?"

"Yes, bro," said Cane. "We'll make your life hell and that twin brother of yours with another stupid name, Sebastian."

Sparks seemed to know that something was wrong and sidled up beside Flick.

"Look at that old nag!" said Jake. "You the Miss High and Mighty's horse."

"He's not mine. He belongs to the gypsies. Please don't hurt him," begged Flick as Jake went to hit the animal with the butt of his rifle. Sparks, however, was a very intelligent pony and gave the boy a kick which sent him staggering backwards.

That made him really angry.

"Don't you mess with us, rich kid, or you will get hurt," shouted Jake. "One word to anyone that you saw us and you will regret it!"

"Yes, you will regret it," echoed Cane, who seemed quite unable to say much for himself. "Like the other little girl who got in the way!"

Immediately, Jake glowered at Cane and muttered to him to 'shut his gob'. Flick pretended she didn't know what they were talking about. All she wanted to do was to get home safely and talk to the detective inspector. She knew now that somehow the Banks family were implicated in the shooting of Sunshine.

Cane came up very close to Flick's face, and for one awful moment she thought he was going to hit her too with his rifle, but he glowered at her, shook his fist in her face and warned her yet again not to tell anyone she had seen them or it would be the worse for her and her family.

"Even castles can burn down!" were his last threatening words before he and Jake walked off through the copse.

Flick began shaking all over once they had gone. She was scared, really scared by Jake and Cane's threats. If they had shot Sunshine and left her badly injured in the woods, they were quite capable of doing anything. Sparks put his nose into her hand. It was comforting. She mounted him and galloped back home. It was getting dark by the time she reached the stable and began to groom the pony.

Her mother heard the pony's hooves trot over the yard into the stable and was relieved to know Flick was back. She went over to make sure that everything was alright and found her daughter sitting on a bale of hay, sobbing. She realised something was very wrong, but Flick wouldn't calm down and tell her what had happened. She sat herself down next to Flick, cuddling her and waiting until the sobs subsided.

Chapter Sixteen

Flick didn't know what to do. If she told her mum about the Banks boys, then something terrible could happen to her or her family. They were obviously capable of being really callous, or they wouldn't have left Sunshine with a bullet in her head. She thought about Sunshine and also the talk with the inspector and felt she did have a responsibility to pass on what she had learnt, but she was really scared.

Her mum let her sobs subside, then gently tried to ask what had happened to upset her so much. She looked at her mum. She had never kept anything secret from her mum but knew if she told her, then their home could go up in flames.

"Has anyone hurt you, darling?" asked her mum. "Did you see anything terrible? People have said there are ghosts that sometimes walk in the castle grounds. You look like you have seen a ghost!"

"No, I'm all right, Mum. No one has hurt me and I didn't see a ghost, but something happened and I can't really tell you about it. I have been threatened that if I tell anyone then there will be terrible consequences."

"Darling, I won't press you. When you have had time to get over whatever the shock was and think about things, I am sure you will know what the right thing to do is. Have the courage to do what is right. Now, before we go in, I want to say a little prayer and ask the Lord to show you what to do and give you peace."

Flick closed her eyes and was glad her mum had prayed. Things always seemed better after you have prayed, she thought.

They went back to the kitchen and it was about time for the evening meal. Theo was all excited about his hens and Seb had loved playing on his new skateboard in the skate park, so they didn't really notice how quiet Flick was and didn't ask any awkward questions as to why her eyes were red or what she had done with her afternoon. The evening dragged by slowly as the family watched TV together. For once, Flick was looking forward to bed but when the phone rang she nearly jumped out of her chair with fright.

Her mum answered it and she was relieved to hear her say, "Hello, Penny. How are you, darling?" Flick wished her sister was at home; maybe she could have talked with her and got her opinion. Normally, she was able to share everything with Seb, but this secret was different, since Cane was in the same class in school. What was she to do? What was the right thing to do?

Flick found she was unable to sleep. She kept tossing and turning and all the time thinking about the problem. She was glad that the next day was Sunday. At least she didn't have to see those horrible boys as they waited for the bus to school. Normally on Sunday mornings, she went with

Theo and Seb to church, where they had a group called Live Wires which she really enjoyed. All the rest of the Wildlife Society belonged too. Sometimes on a club night, the group came up to the castle as there was a games room in one of the spare stables with snooker and table tennis and a swimming pool. They had made several friends in the group and looked forward to the meetings.

Flick was tired and pale and her mum asked her if she was all right.

"I'm fine, Mum," replied Flick. She wasn't really, but didn't want her mum to fuss or worry. "I'll be ready to go to church in a minute. Are you driving us?"

"Yes, and this morning I'll come to church too, now that all the visitors are gone," answered her mother. Flick looked relieved. She didn't want to walk in case she saw those boys.

At least she felt safe in church. That was one place she didn't think she would see the Banks boys. However, her problem was always in her mind and was made worse when the minister announced that before the young people went to their groups, he wanted everyone to pray for Sunshine. The whole village had been shocked by the news, and the church was packed that morning because people wanted to come and pray for her. The minister asked God to help the police catch whoever had committed such a crime and prayed for Sunshine's complete recovery. That prayer made Flick feel even worse.

In the group she tried to concentrate and take part, but her mind was so fearful. Then her ears pricked up as she heard the leader mention a verse from the psalms. It was as if there was no one else in the room and God was speaking just to her. The verse was: "God has said, 'Never will I leave you, never will I forsake you.' So we say with confidence, 'The Lord is my helper, I will not be afraid. What can man do to me?' Hebrews 13:5b–6."

After church, her mum was talking to the gardener Sid and his wife, Evie. Both of them looked quite upset. Flick left the boys chatting to their friends and went over to her mum.

"We just don't know what to do. It's awful," said Edie. "There is shouting all the time and swearing too. We have lived all our married lives in Little Syding and never had neighbours like these."

"Yes, Edie is afraid even to go outside and put the washing on the line, because she gets verbal abuse shouted at her," said Sid. "And if I go out to try to stick up for her, then they call me things like 'stupid old codger'. It's all very upsetting. Mind you, I feel very sorry for the missus next door. It seems she is shouted at all the time. She always looks afraid and jumps out of her skin if you talk to her.

"The noise from the stereo or whatever they have blasts out until late in the night too, and we are afraid to ask them to turn it down. They have five children. The eldest is apparently in the Young Offenders Institute over at Portland

and the way the other three boys carry on I reckon they'll join him there in due course. They seem to have no respect for anybody. The little girl, like her mother, seems to be as quiet as a mouse and quite browbeaten by the fellows. Her eyes are often red as if she cries a lot too. I wonder if I should tell social services about them."

"Don't do that!" said Flick in alarm.

Her mother turned to her. "What do you mean, Flick? Of course they must be told if a child is at risk!"

"I meant," answered Flick, realising she may have given herself away and didn't want to let Sid and Edie be more worried than they need be. "I meant, they are such bullies, those boys, they might guess it was you who informed and make life even more miserable for you!"

"The boys will just have copied their father," said Edie. "He comes and goes all times of the day and night. Apart from going down to Much Syding pub, I don't know what he does. He doesn't appear to have a regular job, though some days a large car is parked in the drive. I think they came from East London and it must be very quiet for them in our little village," she added, trying to think of something that might excuse the family's behaviour.

"I'm so sorry that life is miserable for you, Edie. Why don't you come and have a coffee when Sid comes to do the garden and we can have a quiet chat?" Sally offered as they began to make their way to the car. She really didn't know how to help her elderly friends.

Flick got in the front seat next to her mother and they waited for the boys to join them.

"Mum," said Flick, "I do have to tell you what happened yesterday, and it's about those boys who live next to Sid and Edie. I need to talk to the inspector too."

"Right, darling," her mum looked relieved. "As soon as we get home I will phone him. I don't know if he works on Sunday. Anyway, you can tell me all about whatever upset you straight after lunch. Here come Seb and Theo, so we'll get home quickly."

Now she had decided to tell, Flick couldn't wait for dinner to be finished. Her mother phoned the inspector as soon as they got in and he promised to come round that afternoon. The boys were wondering what was going on and were very pleased when Flick said to her mother that they could hear what happened.

Although Flick had been so upset and frightened, once she had decided to tell what she knew, she was surprisingly calm and able to explain all that had happened in the copse. The inspector had a little recorder and every now and then asked her gently to explain a little more or repeat what she heard.

At the end, Seb and Theo were both seething with anger that those boys had dared to threaten their sister and they also knew they were probably not idle threats.

"I'm really sorry that I didn't tell you yesterday," Flick said to the inspector. "I was too scared that those bullies would keep their word and burn down our house."

"I understand completely and am very grateful that you found the courage to speak to us. I agree—the threats must be taken seriously, even if they are from schoolboy bullies. I will arrange police protection here at the castle until we get this case wrapped up. That can include escorting you to school, if you like, and I will also speak to the headmaster about the possibility of bullying occurring there. Now I must get to work on the information you have given us."

The inspector left and Sally hugged her daughter. "What made you change your mind?" she asked.

"It was a verse that was read to us in the Live Wires group. It promised that Jesus would never leave us and because of that we didn't have to be afraid or worry about what people might do to us. After hearing that, I knew I should talk about yesterday."

Chapter Seventeen

Seb and Theo walked either side of Flick as they went down the drive to wait for the school bus. Flick had said to the policeman who turned up the evening before to guard them that she would be fine going to school. She had decided to hold her head up high and look the bullies in the eye, for Jesus was with her. In fact, Jake was not there, only Cane, and without his big brother he looked sheepish rather than menacing. Flick gave him a cheery hello, but he glowered at her and turned away. Seb sat beside her on the bus and all was well. Theo sat with Tyler, as usual.

"You'll never guess!" Tyler said excitedly. "Sunshine had all the tubes out yesterday and is up and dressed and playing in the ward! The doctor said she might come home later in the week if all the tests are normal. Even he said it was a miracle that she recovered so well. He was afraid she might have suffered brain damage. He is sure that even the fits will soon stop once the swelling in her brain has gone."

"I'm so glad," answered Theo. "I can't tell you on the bus, but the inspector is making progress finding the culprit. We all have to take care of Flick though, in case she is intimidated as she gave some evidence to the inspector yesterday."

It all sounded very mysterious to Tyler, but he knew his friend well enough to trust him that there must be a very good reason why he wouldn't tell him on the bus. Once they arrived at school, the two 'T's' made sure that Flick got safely to her classroom, then went to theirs. Theo then explained all that had happened over the weekend. Tyler was livid. He wanted to find Cane and tear him apart.

"We have to leave this to the police," said Theo. "We might make everything worse if we try to get revenge. I'm sure everything will be taken care of very soon. Meanwhile, we have police protection at home. Can you believe that! Last night we had a young policeman who came with a beautiful German Shepherd dog and patrolled the castle all night. That will protect my chickens too," he added.

At break, Flick decided to visit the Prayer Space. She hadn't done that before. She wrote her request on a piece of paper and pinned it to the board. Then she sat on the chair provided and took out of her pocket a piece of paper on which she had written out the verse from Hebrews that had spoken to her the day before. She was comforted after reading it and felt she could go into the playground without being afraid. She saw a group of her girlfriends and joined them. They were chatting about ordinary things and when the bell went, they all walked together to the sports hall. The next lesson was gymnastics which Flick loved and she forgot about all her troubles as she did the routines. After she had changed and was making her way to the chemistry lab, she suddenly found herself cornered and face to face with Cane.

"You little cow! I warned you what would happen if you told on us," he said, pushing her against the wall and grabbing her by the hair. "You think you are better than us because you live in a castle and speak with a fancy accent."

Before Flick was able to get her breath, he had grabbed her bag from her shoulder and was throwing everything around, looking for her purse or anything of value.

Suddenly, she remembered she was not on her own and boldly looked the bully in the eye.

"Cane, you are nothing but a big bully. Stop this at once. I will report you." And she pulled out a personal alarm which her mum had given to her to carry and pressed it. Within seconds, help arrived and two teachers released her from Cane's grasp and took him to the headmaster. The school secretary was at her side and looked after her. Somehow she knew that Cane would never trouble her again.

Back at the castle, Sid was busy in the garden, trimming the hedges now that the snow had gone. He had taken up Sally's invitation and brought Edie along with him. So much had happened since they had talked at church the previous day, he knew Edie could do with a good chat.

"You would never believe it," Edie told Sally, "But the police raided our next door neighbours' late yesterday afternoon!" Sally could well believe it, but she kept that to herself and let Edie continue.

"There were uniformed and plain clothes police, and they took the family by surprise. There was a lot of shouting and carrying on, I can tell you. Then they took the father and the two biggest boys to the police station in the police van. They took guns out of the house! After they had gone I heard that poor woman crying, so I went and asked her if she wanted a cup of tea. I made her one and took her some of my home-baked scones and some Christmas cake which we had left. I feel so sorry for her. I reckon she's married to a bad man. Not like my Sid. He wouldn't harm a fly, he wouldn't."

Edie paused to take a sip of her coffee. Then she continued, "Later that night the police brought back the younger of the two boys but have kept the father and the older boy in custody. We've never known such goings on in Lesser Syding before."

"Well, let's hope the police sort it all out," said Sally. "It is difficult having troublesome neighbours." She didn't know quite what else to say, so tried to change the subject and told her the latest news from Penny and then of Sunshine's progress.

Later that day they heard that Jake and his father had been charged for owning shotguns without licenses, poaching, trespassing, endangering life and leaving the scene of a crime. The soles of their trainers had been examined, and Jake's matched the patterns that the girls had drawn. The vehicle tyre marks matched those of a vehicle which the father borrowed several times a week to take away his booty after they had been out poaching. The most important evidence was the empty cartridge which the forensic laboratory proved to have been fired from one of the guns taken from the house.

As threats had been made to Flick that endangered her well-being and that of her family home, the two prisoners were kept in custody and not allowed bail until they had appeared at court.

After the incident at school, it was decided that Cane would also appear before the juvenile court on charges related to his bullying and threatening behaviour. Sid and Edie had also complained about all the noise and rudeness they had put up with, although they didn't want to get the mother into trouble.

Chapter Eighteen

*I*t was a wonderful day when Sunshine was allowed home. In both the Syding villages, people put out banners and balloons, and a large sheet decked the primary school railings which read, "WELCOME HOME, SUNSHINE. WE LOVE YOU." There was a much happier atmosphere too in the neighbourhood since the culprits had been caught. Poaching of pheasants was one thing, but to shoot a small child even by accident and leave her to bleed to death was a terrible crime which people found hard to understand or forgive.

Gran was in her element. She was planning a real Romany feast to welcome home her little granddaughter. Now that the snow had gone, it was not too cold to eat outside in true gypsy style. Sunshine's mum, Betty, had done lots of baking in her oven, making delicious cakes and biscuits, including Sunshine's favourite gingerbread men. Gran would have liked to have invited everyone from Much and Little Syding, but that was not possible, so just the castle family and the Jenkins family had been asked. Fortunately, it was not raining or windy, so everyone wrapped up warm and didn't feel at all cold sitting around the camp fire. Once they had eaten all they could manage the singing began, with Tyler's parents playing violin and guitar. It was such fun to have a winter outdoor party. This one had a special ending because Mr Jenkins had brought a treat, a box of fireworks! He had carefully chosen only colourful ones, none with explosions which could scare Sunshine and remind her of her ordeal. It was a wonderful way to end the celebrations of her homecoming. The only sadness was that Penny was not able to be there, and she was Sunshine's special friend. Flick had a camera and she took some photos to send to her big sister. She hoped they would come out all right even though they were taken in the dark.

The following week seemed quite strange to the children because life had been so eventful ever since Christmas. Now they settled back into the routine of school life and homework. Exams were coming up for the twins, which would determine what options they might take for the next two years. They stayed at school each evening for the homework club and were revising once they were home.

Tyler and Theo started to do their homework together in Theo's turret bedroom, as they had done until Sunshine was hurt. Theo also had to take care of his new hens. They were settling down and beginning to lay. Every night he was very careful to check they were properly shut in and safe from the fox. He and Tyler had shut them in one evening and were going back to the stables to see Sparks when they saw a barn owl perched on a fence post, just looking at them. They were so excited about it, they watched it for some time until it flew away. That was something to put in their nature diaries.

Theo had been very surprised at how much there was to see even in the winter and how early the signs of spring appeared. Until he met Tyler, he had not had any real interest in the environment. Now he loved watching all the wildlife in the countryside. He was even beginning to think he might like to be a farmer when he grew up.

He still loved history, though. Soon the archaeologists were due to arrive and excavate the Roman remains which had been discovered in the castle grounds when the river course was diverted. Perhaps he would be a historian. Thinking about this, Theo realised it had been ages since he and Tyler had taken out the metal detector. They had started to map out all the castle grounds and had intended to explore them section by section, but so many things had happened recently that they had just not done it.

"Ty," suggested Theo, "we've not been out with the metal detector for ages. If it's fine on Saturday, why don't we do that?"

"Good idea!" replied Tyler. "I'd like to go back to Ringstead where we found the pirate's pistol last year. Shall I ask Dad if he'll take us? Actually, do you remember that the curator of the Dorchester Museum said we could watch when the wreck was being excavated? Maybe we should ask when that will be done. I've still got the phone number in my phone."

Tyler found the number and rang the curator who remembered the two 'T's' very well.

"It will probably be the Easter holidays before the wreck is investigated, but don't worry, I have it in my diary to let you know. I haven't forgotten my promise. Let me know when they start the excavations on the Roman site. I should like to see that," the curator said.

"We promise we will. It should be soon, so long as we don't have more snow," replied Tyler.

The following Saturday, Bill was happy to drive the boys to Osmington Mills again so he could let them walk over the rocks carrying their metal detector to where the shipwreck lay. This was just around the cove towards Ringstead. The boys were well wrapped up in anoraks and Wellington boots. The metal detector kept buzzing, but they only found rusty nails and things like that.

It was fun, though, to be out detecting again. This time they were very careful to watch the tide. Last time they had been so excited with their find that they had almost been cut off when the tide turned. They walked back to Osmington Mills and scrambled up the cliff by the Old Smuggler's Inn. Bill was waiting for them in the car park.

"Boys," he said, as soon as they appeared. "I took a walk into the village while you were detecting and there is a cottage which has a notice on it saying they have some kittens to give away to good homes. I reckon that a good home would be Honeysuckle Cottage. Wouldn't Sunshine like a kitten? Shall we go and see if they still have any?"

"Oh, yes!" said Tyler, his eyes shining. "It would be good to have a mouser too. Gran's always complaining about the field mice that get into her stores."

"I wonder if mum would let me have one?" said Theo. "We get mice and worse in the stables. Can I give her a ring?"

Much to his delight, Theo's mum was quite happy for him to get a cat so long as it was an outside pet. It would not be a good idea to have an indoor cat when we have bed and breakfast guests, she explained to Theo, as some people are allergic to them.

Chapter Nineteen

They opened the gate and walked up the path to the cottage. At first, when they rang the bell, it seemed as if no one was in and the boys were very disappointed. Then, they rang a second time and suddenly a little old lady appeared at a side gate.

"Can I help you?" she asked.

"We saw your notice on the gate about kittens," explained Bill. "Do you still have any?"

"Why, yes! Come round the back and I'll show you." She opened the side gate and led them into the back garden. In a shed, she showed the two 'T's' and Bill a basket with the mother cat and three kittens.

"These are all that are left of the litter, one male and two females. They are weaned and ready to leave their mother. Would you like one? I am hoping to find them good homes."

"I think we would like two," said Bill. "Tyler, which do you think Sunshine would like?"

"I am sure she would want a girl," answered Tyler. "Look at that pretty little tabby!" And he picked up the smallest kitten.

"Yes, she's a girl. If she's like her mother, she'll be a good mouser!" commented the old lady.

"I would like a good mouser too," remarked Tyler, "But I would like a male, please."

So the lady picked up the biggest kitten and gave it to Theo. The boys were delighted.

"If you have time to come in, I'll tell you how to look after them," said the old lady. "My cats thrive on lots of love and attention, but they are outdoor cats. Now, how are you going to get them home? Do you live far away?"

"We live in the Sydings, a few miles east of Dorchester," replied Bill. "We have a car, but if you have a cardboard box, it would be very helpful."

The lady took everyone inside her little cottage. It was tiny and they all squashed in the kitchen while she found a box big enough for the two kittens. She put some straw inside and a few nuggets of dry meal. Then she told the boys how to take care of the kittens and sent them on their way.

What a surprise it was when they arrived back at Honeysuckle Cottage. Sunshine was very excited when she was told the kitten was for her. She was not so pleased when she was told firmly that it could not sleep in her room but in the woodshed, because it would grow up to catch mice. Sunshine just called her kitten 'Kitty' and loved it from the moment she saw it.

Bill took Theo home with his kitten. It had very lovely tabby markings. He was really stumped as to what he might call him. Finally, Seb had an idea.

"Let's call him 'Ossie' because you got him at Osmington," he suggested. So 'Ossie' the kitten became. The twins and Theo were enchanted with their new pet. They made a ball and put it on a string and then swung it in front of Ossie, and he kept biffing it with his paw. Their mum found a basket that she lined with an old blanket, and they put it in the stables. She found some newspaper which would have to do as a litter tray until they could get to a pet shop.

Flick quickly rode her bike down to the village shop to buy some cat food before closing time. She hoped the kitten wouldn't miss his mother too much, but he was in the same stable as Sparks, so he would have company.

The kittens soon settled into their new homes and were great fun. It wasn't long before they both became good hunters, which pleased everyone. It helped the children forget some of the horrible things which had happened through January.

After attacking Flick at school, Cane had to face the headmaster, who had a 'zero tolerance' policy towards bullying in his school. Cane wondered if he would be excluded. He had often been excluded from schools in East London, usually for carrying a knife or bullying. If he was excluded from this school, what would he do in the country all day? He missed the town with all its noise and the gang to which he had belonged with his older brothers.

He had been warned when they moved here that it was his final chance to change. His older brother Joe was in the Young Offenders Institution over at Portland, and it looked pretty certain that Jake would end up joining him. Did he really want to go there too? Could things ever be different for him?

In his home people had shouted at him and bullied him for as long as he could remember. Somehow, it was second nature to shout back. His dad was often violent, even towards his mother. Cane wished it could be different. He knew he had been beastly to Flick, but secretly he was jealous of this family who seemed to get on well together and had friends. Cane had never had a special friend. The nearest thing to a friend had been one of the social workers who had kept an eye on him when he was about ten. He had even taught Cane to read, for up until that time he had just messed around in school.

In fact, Cane loved books, but there were none at home to read and once, in London, when he had borrowed one from the library, his brothers had trashed it, so he could never go back and borrow another one.

"I am so ashamed that you have behaved in this way," said the headmaster. "I cannot believe that you have attacked another pupil and more than that, a girl. This school promised to give you one last chance and now you have blown it. What have you to say for yourself?"

Cane looked at his shoes, his face red. He really did feel bad about what he had done, but he felt there was no hope for himself.

"I know you won't believe me, but I am sorry." Suddenly, all his bravado was gone and he felt like crying. He couldn't do that. If ever his London gang got to hear that he snivelled, he'd be thrown out and never live it down.

"I truly don't know what to do with you," said the headmaster. "If I exclude you or expel you, what good will that do? I think I need to discuss this with the school staff and maybe the governors. I am not sure the staff will want you in their classes. I have heard reports of your rudeness. For the time being, you will report to me and I will supervise your lessons here in my study for the next day or so while we decide what to do. I will expect you to give Felicity a formal apology here in my office at the end of the day."

"Yes, sir, thank you, sir," Cane answered politely.

Flick had been very surprised and a bit apprehensive when she was asked to go to the head at the end of the day and even more surprised when Cane had apologised and sounded really sincere. She had been quite upset, but accepted the apology. She knew he would not trouble her again.

Chapter Twenty

*A*fter the court hearing, Cane's father was sent to prison and his older brother to the Young Offenders Institution, because it had been Jake who had fired the gun and both of them had fled the scene of the crime. Jake and his father both had criminal records and the judge felt he could not be lenient. Both had to be sent away.

It was very hard for the rest of the family to continue in the village. Sid and Edie tried to befriend them, but many people ignored them. The headmaster allowed Cane to stay at the school, but he was given a report card and if his behaviour was bad, it was noted on the card and he had to explain himself to the head at the end of the day. He really tried hard not only to behave well, but also to work at his lessons. He was not as stupid as many people thought and without Jake's influence, he started to get on well. Even some of his classmates began to like him and trust him and became friends. Cane was good at football and joined the football club which trained after school. Paul belonged to this too, so the two boys began to talk to each other and even sat together on the school bus.

A few months before, Tyler's father Bill had made friends with a Bulgarian Romany prisoner whom the two 'T's' had found on Portland after he had made an attempt to escape. Ever since, Bill had visited him in the Verne Prison in Portland. Sometimes he took cakes which his wife had baked and sometimes cards which the children had made. He helped him with his English and had written to the prisoner's wife in Bulgaria. Since then Bill had become an authorised prison visitor and regularly went to befriend and help the men in the prison. When he found that Mr Banks who had left his daughter wounded in the woods was admitted to the prison, Bill found he had a problem. He felt he couldn't talk to him or in any way be kind to him, even though he knew he should treat all prisoners in the same way.

One day Edie asked Bill to take some things to the prison for her next door neighbour. He agreed to do that, but knew it would not be easy to face Mr Banks. He knew Jesus said we must forgive the people who hurt us. He kept praying about it, that he would be willing to forgive. The next time he went to the prison, he took the parcel and delivered it. Mr Banks was very uncomfortable and would not look him in the eye. As he gave the parcel to him he quietly said to the prisoner, "I do forgive you for what you did to my daughter Sunshine." Mr Banks looked away and didn't answer. He took the parcel and muttered "Thanks" and disappeared.

As he went home, Bill felt lighter in his heart because he had forgiven Mr Banks. He got home and picked up little Sunshine and swung her around. She squealed with joy.

"Kitty too," she said and he let her down to pick up her kitten and then swung them both around.

He was so thankful that she was strong and well again. What an eventful month January had been! His children always seemed to be caught up in adventures. Maybe February would be quieter and the two 'T's' and all the rest of the gang could keep themselves out of trouble.

Titles available in the Syding Adventures

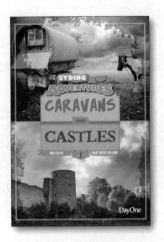

CARAVANS AND CASTLES (1)

Mary Weeks Millard

ISBN 978-1-84625-364-5

PIRATES AND PRISONERS (2)

Mary Weeks Millard

ISBN 978-1-84625-365-2

SUNSHINE AND SNOWSTORMS (3)

Mary Weeks Millard

ISBN 978-1-84625-366-9

Coming soon in the Syding Adventures

ROMANS AND RANSOMS (4)

Mary Weeks Millard

ISBN 978-1-84625-367-6

LIVE WIRES AND LOBSTER POTS (5)

Mary Weeks Millard

ISBN 978-1-84625-368-3

VIKINGS AND VISITORS (6)

Mary Weeks Millard

ISBN 978-1-84625-369-0

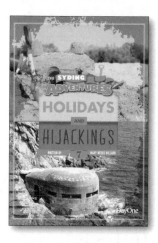

HOLIDAYS AND HIJACKINGS (7)

Mary Weeks Millard

ISBN 978-1-84625-370-6

If you enjoyed these you might like the following books by Mary Weeks Millard

THE SECRET OF THE HIDDEN TUNNEL

Mary Weeks Millard

ISBN 978-1-84625-334-8

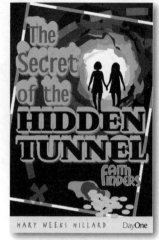

NEVER GIVE UP ON YOUR DREAMS

Mary Weeks Millard

ISBN 978-1-84625-271-6

THE MYSTERY OF THE DESERTED HOUSE

Mary Weeks Millard

ISBN 978-1-84625-272-3

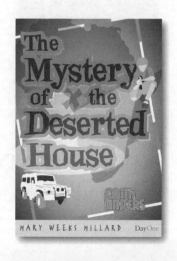